W9-BNO-615

HARLEQUIN®
Presents

In July, escape to a world of beautiful locations, glamorous parties and irresistible men—only with Harlequin Presents!

Lucy Monroe brings you a brilliant new story in her ROYAL BRIDES series, *Forbidden: The Billionaire's Virgin Princess*, where Sebastian can't ignore Lina's provocative innocence! Be sure to look out next month for another royal bride! *The Sicilian's Ruthless Marriage Revenge* is the start of Carole Mortimer's sexy new trilogy, THE SICILIANS. Three Sicilians of aristocratic birth seek passion—at any price! And don't miss *The Greek Tycoon's Convenient Wife* by Sharon Kendrick—the fabulous conclusion to her GREEK BILLIONAIRES' BRIDES duet.

Also this month, there are hot desert nights in Penny Jordan's *The Sheikh's Blackmailed Mistress*, a surprise pregnancy in *The Italian's Secret Baby* by Kim Lawrence, a sexy boss in Helen Brooks's *The Billionaire Boss's Secretary Bride* and an incredible Italian in *Under the Italian's Command* by Susan Stephens. Also be sure to read Robyn Grady's fantastic new novel, *The Australian Millionaire's Love-Child!*

We'd love to hear what you think about Presents. E-mail us at Presents@hmb.co.uk or join in the discussions at www.iheartpresents.com and www.sensationalromance.blogspot.com, where you'll also find more information about books and authors.

ONE NIGHT BABY

When passion leads to pregnancy!

All-consuming attraction...spine-tingling kisses...
unstoppable desire.

With tall, handsome, sexy, gorgeous men like
these, it's easy to get carried away with the
passion of the moment—and end up
unexpectedly, accidentally, shockingly
PREGNANT!

And whether she's his one-night lover,
temporary love-slave at work or permanent
mistress, family life hadn't been in his life
plan—well, not yet, anyway! The sparks will fly,
the passion will ignite and their worlds will be
turned upside down—and that's before the little
bundle of joy has even arrived!

Don't miss any books in this exciting new
miniseries from Harlequin Presents!

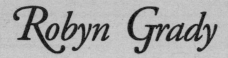

Robyn Grady
THE AUSTRALIAN
MILLIONAIRE'S LOVE-CHILD

❦➤ ONE NIGHT BABY ◄❦

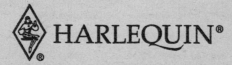

HARLEQUIN®

TORONTO • NEW YORK • LONDON
AMSTERDAM • PARIS • SYDNEY • HAMBURG
STOCKHOLM • ATHENS • TOKYO • MILAN • MADRID
PRAGUE • WARSAW • BUDAPEST • AUCKLAND

ISBN-13: 978-0-373-12746-7
ISBN-10:   0-373-12746-4

THE AUSTRALIAN MILLIONAIRE'S LOVE-CHILD

First North American Publication 2008.

www.eHarlequin.com

Printed in U.S.A.

All about the author...
Robyn Grady

One Christmas long ago, ROBYN GRADY received a copy of *Cinderella* from her big sister, and immediately fell in love. Sprinklings of magic, deepest wishes come true—she was hooked! Picture books with glass slippers later gave way to romance novels, and, more recently, the real-life dream of writing for Harlequin Books.

After a fifteen-year career in television, Robyn met her own modern-day hero. They live on Australia's Sunshine Coast with their three little princesses, two poodles and a cat called Tinkie. Robyn loves new shoes, worn jeans, lunches at Moffat Beach and hanging out with her friends on eHarlequin. Learn about her latest releases at www.robyngrady.com, and don't forget to say hi. She'd love to hear from you!

For Tabitha, Holly and Ashleigh—
dream big, stay strong, be happy.

CHAPTER ONE

'WOULD all the eligible ladies please move to the centre of the room? The bride will now throw the bouquet!'

Sophie Gruebella's gaze jumped from her fingertip, slowly rimming her glass, to the middle-aged DJ, then over to the women jostling for position on the Sydney ballroom dance floor. Her emerald-green gown rustled as she sat up straight and set her hands resolutely in her lap.

Uh-uh. No way. She was pleased her friend had found Mr Right. Wendy and Noah looked perfect together, particularly now, as he brushed a kiss over his wife's lips and Wendy swished her snow-white train out of the way, preparing to lob her roses into the excited skirted throng. But sadly, as far as Sophie was concerned, showing up today had been effort enough.

Practically everyone here knew she'd been unceremoniously dumped three months earlier. Self-medication consisted of a nightly overdose of anything resembling chocolate, and a cycle of romantic comedy DVDs, the happy endings of which made her all the more morose. She'd gained ten pounds—and that was only under her eyes.

The humiliation of being tossed aside for a younger, thinner, more attractive woman was gradually losing its sting; she no longer considered herself in love with Ted, thank heaven. However, being the unassuming rather than assertive type, the blow to her self-esteem had been crushing. The notion of ever falling in love again, let alone literally *chasing* a wedding bouquet, left her feeling ill.

The DJ's dulcet tones resonated around the ballroom, which was decorated with the finest linen and flickering candelabra. 'Last chance, ladies. Who will catch the bouquet? Who's next in line?'

Sophie sighed. Would the happiness Wendy and Noah shared today ever be hers? Could she bear to open up and risk her heart again? Though it pained her to admit it, as more time passed, the less she believed. And heaven knew an extravagant ceremony and a licence were no guarantee any rainbow would last for ever.

As Sophie pondered, a striking masculine figure crossed her path. Her heartbeat skipped, and for a giddy moment that sick feeling in her stomach faded. Handsome in a dangerous 007 kind of way, he stopped slightly ahead and to the right of her. The tuxedo jacket, which emphasised the breadth of his shoulders, shifted as he retrieved a phone from his breast pocket. Profile earnest, long legs braced apart, he checked his watch, shook his head and, after a few indecipherable words into the cellphone, terminated the conversation.

A business call? Odd for a Saturday night. Sophie surveyed the room. His girlfriend must be among that mob limbering up. Because confident, killer-sexy guys like that *always* had girlfriends—and not well-padded, down-hearted specimens like herself.

Sophie pushed her glass aside.

In fact, it was high time she left.

As she scooped the last heart-shaped chocolate into her handbag, a collective whoop went up to the ceiling and something bright and fragrant landed in her lap. She looked down and gasped.

How on earth had Wendy's bouquet flown all the way back here? More importantly—*oh, Lord*—where could she hide?

With every eye drilled upon her, Sophie withered in her seat and the DJ hooted. 'Great throw, Wendy! Let's put our hands together for the shy little lady up the back.'

Over a smattering of applause, Sophie executed a wobbly smile. Even sent a little wave. When the show was finally over, and couples began to re-unite, her friends Penny Newly and Kate Tigress hurried over.

Above the plunging neckline of a silver-sequinned gown, Penny's mouth twisted on a pout. 'I don't get it. Why would you want to catch the bouquet?'

Kate slapped Penny's arm. 'Don't be mean.'

Penny winced and rubbed the spot. 'I only meant that she's single at the moment. It's a bit of a waste.'

As far back as high school, Penny had been known for her beautiful blonde mane, ample bosom and lack of tact. However…

Sophie exhaled. 'You're right. I'm the least likely to marry next.'

Kate sat down and squeezed Sophie's hand. 'You'll get back in the game, Soph. You'll find your soul mate. A man so well suited he'll practically be your twin.'

Sophie found a self-deprecating smile. 'Can we organise a twin without my spare tyre and tangle of hair?'

Preferably someone sleek and *built*.

Past Kate's shoulder, Sophie watched 007 frown into the crowd as he folded impressive arms over an equally impressive chest. Sophie frowned too. Where was the girlfriend?

A skilled hairdresser, Kate swept back a curl which had escaped from Sophie's upsweep. 'Just for the record, your cappuccino curls are gorgeous. And if you cut even an inch, you'll answer to me.' Her playful scowl eased. 'You should flaunt what you have, instead of always trying to hold it back.'

Penny shrugged on a nod. 'And once your clothes fit again…' She came as close as Penny could to offering a sympathetic face. 'Well, you've always been quite pretty. *Really*.'

Kate shot Penny a daggers look at the same time as the music kicked off again and their respective boyfriends—brothers they'd met a month earlier—arrived to whisk both away for a romantic cheek-to-cheek.

Sophie gnawed her lower lip, refusing to give in to the tears prickling at the backs of her eyes. Kate meant well, but Sophie didn't want her pity. And, frankly, she was over wallowing in her own.

Yes, she'd recently limped away from her only long-term relationship. No, she wasn't Miss World. Truth was she might *never* find her true love, the man destined to sweep her off her feet. Lots of people didn't. Maybe, rather than the wedding-bell toll of tradition, she was meant to follow her own beat.

And, heck, perhaps that wasn't such a bad thing. Looking back now, she could see that the Sophie who'd been with Ted was a pale imitation of the woman she wanted to be. She'd been a shadow. An appendage who'd nodded and never made waves. Story of her life, really.

But no more. Starting now, this *minute*, she wouldn't fall back from speaking her own mind. Surely the last thing she needed was a husband setting her boundaries, making the rules?

On a burst of adrenaline, Sophie pushed up out of the chair. She was done worrying over what other people thought—Penny Newly doubly so.

She hadn't taken two steps towards the exit before a hand on her elbow held her back. Puzzled, she pivoted around. She craned her neck back and her stomach looped the loop at the pair of diamond-blue eyes smiling down at her.

The man with the phone, and the shoulders and the chest, pressed the bouquet into her hand. 'You dropped this.'

As she absorbed the heat of his fingers curled over hers, his deep voice—a blend of steel and richest sable—vibrated through her. When his gaze slid to her mouth, the ground shifted beneath her feet and the room began a slow spin.

Thankfully, before she could make a complete fool of herself, Sophie's brain decided to work.

He'd seen the flowers fall from her lap when she'd stood. He was merely being a gentleman, filling in time.

Managing an unaffected smile, Sophie urged the flowers back. 'You keep them. For your girlfriend.' *Or your wife.*

'I'm unattached.' He took the bouquet and blindly set it on the tabletop. 'In fact, I wondered if you'd like this dance.'

Sophie blinked, then stole a wary glance around the room. This man was so out of her league. Was this some kind of joke? But when she met his gaze again, the sexual awareness that had started with a touch began to pour through her veins like thick warm cream.

Hooked by those eyes, she lifted one shoulder and let it drop. 'I was about to leave.'

Claiming her hand, he spoke over a shoulder as he escorted her away. 'Then I'm fortunate I caught you in time.'

Only upon reaching the middle of the floor did he

fold her into the circle of his highly capable arms. Without another word he set a large palm against her back and began to dance.

Conscious of how her feet moved, as if programmed to follow his lead, she let herself relax against the hard plateau beneath his dress shirt and soak up the fresh, hot scent. When his thumb grazed the back of her hand she bit her lip as parched kindling sparked low in her belly.

Her eyes drifted shut.

Don't get excited. This is just a dance.

His deep voice hummed near her ear. 'Your dress is lovely.'

Her cheek all but resting against his shoulder, she melted a little more. 'It's been a while since I wore it last.' She shunted aside a vision of Jolly Green Giant satin stretched over her behind.

Yet he liked her dress. Had her luck changed? And to this extent? She was certain they hadn't met before. Had Noah ever made mention of this man? A work colleague from the bank, perhaps?

And why was she even asking herself these questions? She was supposed to be off men.

At least she kind of remembered thinking something like that…

Her dance partner picked up the conversational thread. 'Black tie isn't a weekly dress requirement for most people.'

Maybe not. Still… 'That tuxedo doesn't look so out of place on you.'

'It gets a decent workout. Hasn't seen a wedding in a while, though. It's been a nice day, with the church ceremony and the speeches—' he whirled her around in a flawless move '—the bridal waltz.'

Yep—all perfect. Right down to the hired Rolls-Royce. She scanned the opulent ballroom, wrapped in silk bows, glowing light and soft music. 'It must have cost of fortune.'

'I'm sure Noah thinks it's worth every cent.'

'Wendy too.' With both sets of parents passed away, she and Noah had covered all the expenses. Wendy's designer gown alone had cost thousands.

His voice lowered. 'You sound unconvinced. Don't you think a traditional day with all the trimmings is worth the expense?'

She pressed her lips together. 'Not my place to say. It's not my day.'

'And if it was your day?'

She suppressed a sigh, wishing she could feel as enthusiastic as she should for the deserving couple. A few moments ago she'd made a vow to lift herself out of her sadsack hole. Even given the benefit of her mystery man's unexpected attention and this wonderful dance, she guessed she still had a way to go.

She shook her head. 'I'm not the person to ask right now.'

'Because of what your thoughtless friend said a moment ago?'

As his words sank in, her stomach flipped. She searched those hypnotic blue eyes. Did she have it right? It hurt to even say it. 'You overheard that conversation?'

One dark brow arched. 'I heard enough.'

Once your clothes fit again... Quite pretty. Really. Bit of a waste...

Her throat convulsed on rising humiliation and her cheeks flamed for a second time that night. She cringed, imagining the 'L' burning into her forehead. 'Is that why you asked me to dance? You felt *sorry* for me?'

His lower lip jutted slightly. 'At first. Until I looked more closely.'

She blinked. Was that another compliment? Was the heat she imagined surging between them real?

'And now?' she asked.

The hand on her back manoeuvred her closer. 'I answered your question. Your turn to answer mine. How do you envisage your perfect wedding day?'

He held her with his gaze, defying her not to answer, and—dammit—she backed down. But not in the compliant way she might have in the past. She might feel like a dream in this man's arms, but she couldn't forget that foremost it was pity that had landed her here. Frumpy, unfortunate, wallflower Sophie. She was so sick of seeing herself that way, worrying about how she looked and what people thought—well-meaning hunks included.

Did she want a traditional wedding?

She found her inner strength, lifted her chin and spoke her mind. 'Until tonight I would've said I wanted a big wedding, with a big cake and a big bill.'

His eyes lit. 'That's changed?'

She allowed herself a smile. 'Deep down I've always wanted a wedding on the beach. A party with finger-foods and bare toes digging into cool sand. *If* I ever get married,' she qualified.

'Surely you want a husband? A family?'

So aware of the hard length of his body moving in a seductive rhythm against hers, she assessed his curious expression and threw out the challenge. 'Is it so strange for a woman to admit she might not see herself tying any knots?'

He swayed her around. 'Frankly, yes. It's men, not women, who usually run from any altar.'

'Is that based on your own predilections?'

Was he the playboy type? Hands down, he had all the right equipment.

His shadowed jaw shifted. 'Actually, I have nuptials planned for the near future—complete with the big cake *and* big bill.'

Okay, now she was confused. 'You're unattached, but getting married soon?'

'I have a list of requirements. I simply need to find the woman who fits.'

She coughed out a laugh. 'A list? Are you checking it twice? I mean, you're kidding, right?'

His serious look said not. 'Every day I deal with unhappy couples who married without giving enough thought to long-term compatibility. I devised the list for a clueless client a couple of years back, to help him guard against future mistakes.'

Talk about setting boundaries! She almost pitied his future bride. What kind of person thought it necessary to wield such dispassionate control over something like falling in love? 'What are you? A therapist?'

'Divorce attorney.'

'A divorce attorney with a list?' His expression would have been condescending if it hadn't been so charming. She decided to serve it up straight. 'I don't think I've heard anything less romantic.'

'Try angry people fighting over assets, using children as pawns. Impulsive love, careless marriages—most often they turn to frustration, regret, and sometimes even hate.'

She thought it through and made up her mind. She might feel particularly jaded after the Ted incident, and admittedly she was having real trouble believing in rainbows, however... 'Sorry, but if I had to choose I'd take falling head over heels in love over checklists any day.'

His square jaw hardened and his gaze left hers to drift over the heads in the room. 'In that case, you're right. You shouldn't tie any knots.'

She stiffened.

Not with you, anyway.

After doubling her defences against the steam radiating from his body through to hers, she dished out another observation. 'You'd have to find someone pretty special to go along with a checklist.'

His untroubled gaze swung back to lick her lips. 'Ah, but finding someone special is what it's all about.'

As she tried to push their difference of opinion from her mind his hips seemed to press closer, and the spark in her belly leapt higher. Sophie dropped her chin as her eyes drifted closed against the threat of unbidden pleasure and mounting frustration.

Should she even try to respect this man's clinical viewpoint? Normally manners and 'what was expected' would win out, but when that bouquet had fallen from her lap tonight something had changed. She'd turned a corner, grown taller, broken free, and now, no matter what, she couldn't go back to being a mouse. She simply couldn't do what decorum required and let this rest.

When her gaze skewered his again, he didn't appear the least surprised.

'So, if you fell madly in love,' she said, 'but she got, say, three strikes on your list, she'd be out of the door?'

'A parting of the ways would be best. The relationship simply wouldn't survive long-term.'

She and Ted had liked many of the same things. Her parents had started out sharing interests. Now they barely spoke. On the other hand, her nan and grandpa had zilch in common, yet they still looked at each other all gooey and held hands walking down the street.

Common interests. No common interests. This man's logic was obviously flawed, and she was going to tell him.

She gave him a level look. 'I think finding the right one is more about luck than arrangement.'

Crisp black fabric brushed beneath her fingers as he rolled back a shoulder. 'Your prerogative.'

She pressed her lips together. No, she wouldn't ask. She'd bite off her tongue before giving him the satisfaction.

She set her teeth, but the question escaped anyway. 'What's at the top of your list?'

He pinned her with a mock stern glare. 'Someone who won't argue.'

That settled it. *GQ* material or not, clearly he rubbed her the wrong way. Why prolong the aggravation? She'd make it easy for them both.

After disengaging herself, she stepped back, straining to keep her voice even. 'Guess you asked the wrong girl to dance.'

His head cocked. 'Why? Because we have opposite ideas on how a couple should meet, court, then celebrate their union—in fact, pretty much everything there is to securing a lifelong companion?'

Ridiculous. She'd known him barely ten minutes, yet her silly heart squeezed as she nodded.

A smile curved a corner of his mouth as he scratched his temple. 'Trouble is, I enjoyed our dance.' When he stepped into the space separating them, her body responded with a knee-quaking wave of warmth. 'But it was just a dance. No budding romance. No broken hearts. No harm done.'

Sophie finally released the air burning in her lungs. Oh, hell. She hated to admit it, but he was right. She'd been on a razor-sharp edge all night, and while the idea of his list irked, she had no need to throw down her glove. That was his business, not hers. The new assertive Sophie needed time to adjust.

His expression softened as he held out a hand. 'Truce?'

She succumbed to a small smile. 'Sure. Why not?'

She imagined his hand held hers a moment longer than was necessary before his chest inflated and he nodded towards the doors behind her.

'I need some fresh air. Care to join me on the balcony?' His mouth twitched. 'On a purely platonic basis, of course.'

Sophie hesitated, then saw the humour shining in his eyes.

Should she join him on the balcony? She would never be affected by his list; he couldn't impose any boundaries on her. But, irrespective of his quirks, this man's company was the most stimulating she'd ever had. If he had nothing better to do, heaven knew neither did she. And after the last few heated moments some fresh air would be nice. A rerun of *The Wedding Date* could wait.

They mounted three stairs and, after passing through a set of wall-to-wall French doors, left the party noise and dressed tables behind. Crossing the patio, adorned with trellises of perfumed lemon and maroon hibiscus, they moved towards a view that included the twinkling rainbow of lights decorating Sydney's coat-hanger bridge. He leant back against the sculptured stone railing, crossed his arms and met her gaze.

A steady pulse beat in his jaw while a lock of hair bounced on the salty autumn breeze drifting in off the glimmering harbour. Sophie's heartbeat hitched. Even if he was insufferably superior, she had to concede James Bond had zip on this guy.

She looped her loose spiral of hair behind an ear. 'When did you decide you wanted to get married?'

'Tonight.'

She hiked a brow. 'This from a guy who won't act on impulse?'

His sexy grin said, *Touché*. 'I've known Noah since school. We lost touch until recently. Seeing him get settled made me realise I'm not getting any younger. I want a wife. A son. It's time.' He turned to face the view and rest his forearms on the railing. 'And you? I'm sure at some stage you want children.'

Hands cushioning the small of her back, Sophie leant against the railing. Normally she wouldn't consider discussing such intimate matters with a stranger. After a year's dating, she and Ted hadn't even touched upon the subject of rattles and playpens.

But hadn't she decided not to be a shrinking violet? What possible harm could come from a little sharing? In fact, she'd bottled so much up from her friends and colleagues over these last three months it would be a relief to let some of it go.

'I love kids.' It was a big reason she'd become a schoolteacher. 'I always thought when the time was right, when I found the right one...' Her voice trailed off.

When? Or did she mean *if?*

One thing she did know: she would never say *I do* unless she was totally, one hundred per cent certain of an unshakable love: no compromise. And right now, miserable though it might sound, she couldn't see it anywhere in her near future.

Shifting to hug herself against the chill in the air, she tried to make light. 'Guess I'll put any plans for a family on the backburner.'

'While I bring it to the front.' His voice lowered. 'Seems we're at odds again.'

Her arms dropped and she pushed off the rail. She'd had enough air. 'If I think of anyone who might help, I'll send her on. Thanks for the dance.'

He spun around. 'Where are you going?'

'Time to call it a night.' The last of the Cadbury's block in her chocolate bin beckoned. Come Monday she'd join the gym. Maybe a new body would help reinforce a new frame of mind.

She started off, but his disapproving tone pulled her up. 'You're going to let them see you walk out of here alone?'

Puzzled, she shrugged. 'That was always going to happen.'

'There is an alternative.'

She read his mind and shuddered. No more pity, *please*. 'You don't have to escort me out.'

He sauntered forward, his dynamic silhouette breathtaking in the slanted moonlight. 'I had something a little more eye-catching in mind.'

She waved her hands. 'Whatever it was, I've had enough attention heaped on me tonight.'

His tall, athletic frame backed her up towards the doors. Moving in reverse, she swallowed, wondering at the devilish look stealing across his face. 'What were you planning?'

He grinned. 'Sweet revenge.'

The moment they re-entered the room, he swept her up into the powerful bands of his arms and the air left her lungs in a shriek. She was weightless! Floating high above the usual normality of her world. It must be a dream. Things like this didn't happen to her. Soon the alarm would go off.

A nervous laugh spilled out. *'What are you doing?'*

'Giving your friend an exit to remember. She can stick *this* in the back of her yearbook.'

It clicked. 'You're going to carry me out in front of everyone?'

He looked disappointed. 'That's only half of it.'

Parading themselves certainly made an impression. A Mexican wave erupted across the room as, one by one, the crowd turned to gape at the picture they must have created—she nestled in her knight's arms like a rescued damsel, gauzy curtains billowing all around. Standing together with their boyfriends, Penny and Kate gazed on, frozen in awe like life-size garden statues. Kate began to smile.

When they had everyone's attention, and even the music had died, her modern-day Sir Galahad descended each step, not once looking down or cracking a smile. As he moved forward the wedding guests parted—a wheat field divided by the hot blast of a breeze.

Not certain how she should react, but helpless not to relish every moment, Sophie linked her arms around his neck and whispered, 'What am I supposed to tell them later?'

With no word of warning, he stopped and dropped his mouth over hers.

He kissed her so deeply, so thoroughly, jets of colour-filled fireworks exploded in her head. When their lips softly parted, she was vaguely aware of their audience and a round of booming applause. Bowled over, she melted into the rocking motion as he started out again.

'Tell them you only used me for sex,' he said as they left the room, 'and that I'm the biggest notch on your bedpost yet.'

CHAPTER TWO

COOPER SMITH stopped into the deserted hotel corridor outside a pair of metallic lift doors. He shucked back his shoulders, then considered the stunned package cradled in his arms.

He grinned. 'I think they enjoyed the show.'

God knows he had. That exit had been the first entirely wild thing he'd done in ages. He'd read somewhere that breaking loose every so often was a tonic for the soul. He had a feeling it could also be highly addictive, which—given his professional knowledge about impulsive behaviour—was probably not a good thing.

She took him in, big green eyes luminous with shock. He was starting to wonder if it might be permanent when she smiled, then began to laugh. Her jiggling body, that infectious sound—he had to chuckle too.

Eyes watery with effort, she finally got her breath. 'I bet Penny's jaw is still on the floor.' She shook her head in astonishment. 'I can't believe we just did that.' Then she frowned. 'I can't believe you didn't warn me.'

'You'd only have argued.'

She dealt him that haughty look. 'Maybe not.'

If anything she was consistent.

Consistently disagreeable.

Normally he wouldn't get involved, but the sight of an attractive woman on her own, a colourful bouquet sitting like a death sentence in her lap, had reeled him in. His heartstrings had tugged him all the way into asking her to dance. That he'd enjoyed their time together was a bonus, even after her stubborn streak had made it crystal-clear she most definitely was not 'the one'.

She wasn't an advocate of tradition, marriage or, it seemed, even having a family. Most alarming...she believed a successful union was based on *luck*. A time bomb waiting to explode. He needed someone who looked at life and love level-headedly.

A person made his own luck.

Still, regardless of their differences, despite the fact there could be nothing between them, he couldn't regret that kiss. Not that it would happen again.

He inspected the closed lift doors. 'So, up or down?'

'To the lobby and a taxi...so, down.'

Adrenaline was pumping through his body, bunching his muscles, firing the synapses over his skin. He wasn't the least bit tired. They couldn't go back to work off their energies at the wedding reception, however.

'It's too early to go home.'

'It's almost eleven.'

Hardly late. 'Are you tired?'

Her mouth twisted to one side. 'I thought I was.'

Solution. 'Join me for coffee.'

'I don't drink coffee.'

He raised a brow. How could he forget? If he wanted to walk left, she would insist they go right.

He persisted. 'Something cool, then?'

'Tell you what, put me down and I'll think about it.'

Cooper paused, then cleared his throat. How had that detail slipped his mind?

He lowered her and she brushed off her gown. Her scent lingered—cinnamon and perhaps vanilla, a combination of spicy and sweet that suited her down to the ground.

A spiral of hair spilled across her heart-shaped face as she angled her head to study him. 'I'll be honest. I don't know how to take that invitation.'

On the surface it might look like more pity, or an attempt to slip that notch on his bedpost, or, at best, a waste of time. But it was much simpler than that. Maybe it was seeing his friend happily married, but if she was feeling a little lonely tonight, so was he.

He scooped his hands into his pockets.

Of course, a more rational explanation was that he'd been working too hard for too long. But all that was too much information.

'We know we're not suited in a romantic sense, so you needn't worry that we'll somehow fall into bed.' Hurt flooded her eyes and he inwardly cringed.

Damn. And he'd thought her friend was tactless. He pushed on. 'We'd just be two responsible adults, who have mutual friends, sharing a drink and some conversation after a wedding.'

A faint line formed between her brows. She nibbled her lower lip and studied him.

He withdrew his hands from his pockets. 'Or I can ride with you down to the ground floor and see you get a cab.'

The doubt in her face faded. She had the most exquisitely shaped lips—soft, luscious, made for kissing, not warring. But that was getting off-track.

She tipped her head. 'There's a coffee shop off the lobby. Guess I could enjoy one quick hot chocolate on the way out.'

Surprised, but pleased, he thumbed the lift button. 'One quick one it is.'

An elderly lady appeared and squeezed between them to hit the 'up' arrow. 'That shop closes at ten,' she told them, rearranging a cerise shawl around a pair of robust shoulders. 'If you're after hot chocolate, I recommend Room Service. Best I've tasted.'

A lift arrived, and the lady disappeared behind the doors. At the same time the next lift pinged… going down.

Cooper scrubbed his jaw. 'Guess that does that.'

'You have something against Room Service?'

He looked at her hard. He must have it wrong. 'Are you saying you'd come to my room?'

'Depends. Do you have one?'

'As a matter of fact, I do.' Despite his attempt at blasé, surprise must have shown on his face.

'We're both over twenty-one,' she pointed out calmly. 'Besides, you just finished telling me seduction is the last thing on your mind. In case you're worried, the same goes for me.'

He grinned at her impudent look. Or was it saucy? If she wasn't such a pain in the rear end…

But she was right. He had a plan. A list. Now it was set in his mind, nothing would dissuade or distract him. He wouldn't seduce her, though others might. He constantly cautioned his kid sister to be careful. Guys loved sex. Most would do almost anything to get it. And plenty ran a sprinter's mile if precautions failed and suddenly baby made three.

A couple of minutes later they arrived at the penthouse floor and he let her into the apartment. She crossed the Italian marble floor to sample the expansive harbour view that featured the Opera House's majestic shells.

'You reserved a whole loft apartment for the night?' she asked, moving to the far wall to inspect his favourite painting—a warm, brightly hued abstract he'd picked up in Hanoi. 'Must've cost a packet.'

He shucked out of his jacket and hung it on the hall stand. 'I own it.'

'Oh, you do not.' Her sceptical face slid. 'In this hotel?'

Making his way to the expansive black granite wet bar, he nodded.

'This is the sort of space I imagine movie stars hire,' she murmured, taking it all in. 'Do you actually live here?'

He picked up the bar's phone extension. 'I have a house in the northern suburbs.'

Making herself at home, she folded into the couch, the emerald of her gown striking against the beige suede cushions. His gaze skimmed her hair.

What would those upswept dark waves look like dancing around her shoulders? Stunning, would be his guess. Long and bouncy.

'I bet it's big?'

With a start, his mind skipped back. The line connecting him to Room Service rang in his ear. 'Excuse me?'

'Your house,' she said. 'I bet it's big.'

The agent had described it as a mansion, but it was more an investment—like this double-storey loft. 'It's comfortable.'

He ordered their drinks, then poured two ice waters.

Her grin was knowing. 'You look like you come from money.'

He hadn't thought about it. 'My parents were well off, but far from rich. When they died, five years ago, I had to provide for my younger sister. So I pumped more energy into my law firm and at the same time invested well. Shares, bonds, property. The usual portfolio.'

'You must have lucked out on some great choices along the way.'

Luck had had little to do with it. His success was based on good planning.

Frowning, he moved to join her. 'You have a real thing with superstition, don't you?'

'Only about certain things.'

'For instance?'

'Spilt salt. You have to throw it back over your left shoulder for good luck.'

'What about black cats?'

'They bring good luck. Even better if you stroke their head three times.'

Stopping before her, he laughed. 'You honestly believe that?'

'King Charles I of England loved his black cat and had it guarded every minute. The very day after it died he was arrested and later beheaded for treason. Thank you…' Accepting her water, she tilted her head at him. 'I don't even know your name.'

Easing down beside her, he pulled loose his black bow tie. 'Cooper Smith. Yours?'

She swallowed a mouthful. 'Sophie will do. I hate my last name.'

'Couldn't be any worse than Smith.'

'That's a note from heaven compared to mine.' She heeled off her silver stilettos and wiggled two sets of dainty toes. Painted deep red. Very nice—particularly against her creamy skin. 'My mother said not to worry because I could dump it when I got married.'

A feat she wasn't certain of accomplishing now.

He put her toes, and marriage, from his mind and

eased back into the cushions. 'You could change your name by deed poll.'

'A bit drastic, don't you think?'

He grunted. Had she agreed with *anything* he'd said tonight? Pity the poor fool who fell in love with her. She'd have him hopping all over the place.

'Statistics confirm both men and women are waiting longer to marry.' He hid a wry grin behind his glass. 'So you might get lucky yet.'

She smiled sweetly. 'So might you.'

Like an avalanche, the memory of his mouth covering hers suddenly crashed the cells of his body and his mind. He rubbed his eyes with an index finger and thumb. Obviously he was more tired than he'd thought. He had been up past two last night, going over some briefs for a big court case next week.

Professions. Yes, that was safe subject.

His stretched out his legs and crossed them at the ankles. 'So, you know I'm a lawyer. What do *you* do for a living, Sophie Last-name-withheld?'

'I'm a schoolteacher, and love it.' She smiled as if she had a secret. 'Well, most days.' Hooking an arm behind her over the couch, she sighed at the ceiling. 'Teenage girls can be so single-minded.'

He raised his brows. Tell him about it. He had one at home, always trying to bend the rules. Not in his house.

'Half are great with homework and focusing,' she continued. 'All the other half think of is playing house and having babies.'

As she spoke, his gaze ran over her… Big green eyes, pert little nose, flawless skin. Feeling every inch like a rippling touch—around her face, up her arm—a bright-tipped wave reeled over him. Tingling.

Hot.

He shifted and sat taller. More residual effects from that kiss. Nothing he couldn't handle if he put his mind to it. She was attractive—sexy, even—but no one to become romantically involved with. Absolutely not. He had a list, a plan, and someone with Sophie's traits was exempt.

He cleared the thickness from his throat. 'Your students…do they come to you for advice?' He used to have a favourite teacher he'd confided in. Paige, his sister, had mentioned one too.

Sophie nodded. 'One girl in particular. She's a darling—sixteen—and I think her boyfriend must be putting the hard word on her.'

Paige was sixteen, but thankfully no boyfriend dominated the scene. Because Cooper knew all about teenage boys—virile, myopic, bursting with testosterone. But honestly, when all was said and done… 'I guess you can't blame boys for constantly thinking about…'

Thinking about…

Sex. Dammit, they were thinking about sex. He was thinking about it now. The slope of Sophie's throat, the rise of her breasts, that silver charm bracelet on her left wrist winking in the light, as if beckoning.

Tensing every muscle, he dropped his focus to the glass he now held tight enough to break.

For God's sake, Smith, snap out of it! Get your mind out of the bedroom.

Sophie's raised arm fell onto her lap. 'I understand that human beings are built that way. Hormones, raging sexual cravings to get close…so close you're practically living in each other's skin—' Her gaze cut back to him and she tipped forward, frowning. 'Are you all right? You look uncomfortable. Are you hot?' She flipped a finger at his collar. 'You should undo that top button.'

With adrenaline pumping a million to one beneath his ribs, his next words came out strangled. 'I think I'll leave it fastened.'

Her concerned gaze skated over his brow. 'You might be coming down with something. A horrible flu ripped through my school last week. One minute you're fine, the next you're flat on your back.'

She leant closer and his blood began to sizzle. He didn't need to hear about anyone being on their back.

'A cold compress might help.' She thought for a second, then slid her cool glass over his brow. 'Better?'

He groaned. *Oh, dear Lord, yes.*

Closing his eyes, he dissolved against the sensation of hot against cold. Her soft body inches from his hard one. He wondered if she would guess his thoughts…how she'd react…what she'd feel like under that dress.

His eyes sprang open.

Enough, already!

As he jumped back his arm bumped hers, and water splashed a cold patch on his crotch. He sprang to his feet at the same time she sprang to hers.

Automatically she brushed his wet trousers, then realised what she was doing. Not that he minded her hands-on attention—not one bit.

Stepping back, she blinked at him several times as a moment of blinding understanding and aware-ness flashed between them. His gaze ended on her lips, which she wet nervously before announcing, 'I should go.'

It was the wedding, the talk about sex, the memory of that sensational kiss. *That* explained why he felt this kind of attraction—hard, fast, totally unrea-sonable. It had crept up on him like a cat on a mouse. A lucky black cat with big green eyes.

She moved to leave, but his hand snapped out to grasp her charm braceleted wrist. She turned back slowly, chest rising and falling as if she couldn't get enough air. Mirrored in her eyes he saw the same desire he felt surging through his veins. Right or wrong—possibly both—he had to act.

'I don't want you to go.' Seemed he'd been saying that all night. This minute he meant it more than ever.

Her slender throat bobbed as she swallowed. 'Why?'

He ground out, 'You know why.'

He felt her holding her breath, evaluating the situa-tion, going over their conversations. Her words came out a threadbare whisper. 'We weren't going to do this.'

'I changed my mind.' He had no other explanation. 'I think you might have too.'

To test his theory, he skimmed a palm up the silken texture of her arm and those earlier tingles caught light. When she didn't move, he slid that hand around her waist. She examined the motion, then searched his eyes while her own glistened in the soft light. 'We're totally incompatible.'

As if drawn by a magnet, he lowered his head to touch her lips oh-so-softly with his. Physical longing curled like a fist in his stomach. 'Without a word of a lie, right now I only remember how you taste.'

When his mouth met hers again, she kissed him back. As he pulled away, her eyes drifted open. Her sigh was a sound near surrender. 'I remember too.'

He tugged her closer and her body melded with his—supple, curvaceous, inviting. Nose touching hers, he murmured against her lips, 'I want you to know I didn't intend for this to happen.'

She looked both anxious and decided. 'This is purely physical, right?'

Yes. 'Purely physical.' Overpowering, irresistible. No *for ever* tied in romantic ribbon here.

'We're agreed. We won't pursue this. I'm not what you want. You're not what I need. We have no future.'

'But we can have tonight.'

The next kiss left his breathing ragged and left her clinging to his shirt like a lifebuoy. He went in deep, feeling his pulse rate spike, his energies harden, knowing, regardless of what was said next, there was no turning back.

When he let her surface, she was looking over his shoulder, a little amazed. 'Cooper, you have a painting of butterflies on the wall.'

Tasting her temple, he carefully released the zip down her back. 'Do I?' He couldn't remember.

'Three white butterflies together. That's very good luck.'

'Have you heard the saying, make love three times before dawn and your life will be long and happy?'

She grinned. 'Think that's true?'

'Only one way to find out.' For a second time that night, he swept her up into his arms.

Their eyes remained glued as he carried her up to his master bedroom.

'When I first saw you,' she murmured, 'I thought you looked dangerous.'

'And now?'

She touched his cheek. 'Now I need to know for sure.'

CHAPTER THREE

WHEN they reached the bedroom, Cooper nudged a light switch with his elbow and the glow from a corner lamp faded up. Sophie's breath caught in her chest as he smiled down at her slung in his arms, lidded eyes compelling and hot.

Neither had planned this. When she'd agreed to accompany him to his room she'd believed they both meant what they'd said. Cooper had made it clear she didn't fit his requirements. She'd made it just as clear she considered his attitude towards finding a match puritanical. She was through with overbearing men, and one thing she'd learned about Cooper in their short acquaintance was that he absolutely wanted to be boss.

Yet their bodies had overwritten their concerns and made up their minds for them. In the end Cooper Smith's unique and potent brand of sex appeal was simply too convincing to resist. What he saw in her she couldn't say. This had never happened before—not even in her dreams. Was it a by-product of her assertiveness when they'd danced—her decision to speak up rather than suppress? How had Kate put it? 'You should flaunt what you have, instead of always trying to hold it back.'

Either way, being desired by a sexy, powerful man was flattering. Now she was here, she wouldn't back down. Rather, she would enjoy every stimulating moment. Tonight, for the first time, she would completely lose herself and reach for a handful of far-flung stars.

And tomorrow she would have no regrets. The only consequence would be a boost to her confidence. God knew, it was time.

He carried her to the side of an ominous-looking king-sized bed, then carefully angled her to set her on her feet. Cupping her cheek, he dropped the most tender of kisses at one side of her mouth. His attention drifted to her shoulder, and the slide of his hand helped the strap fall to her elbow. 'I should cancel the hot chocolates.'

As his kiss tasted her lips more fully, and the other strap fell too, delicious warmth flooded her belly and seeped through her limbs. She didn't want him to temper the mood by picking up the phone.

With the zip already undone, the dress dropped in a rustling puddle at her feet. She shivered as the air, enhanced by his mesmerising masculine scent, brushed her breasts. She felt exposed, vulnerable, yet at the same time smouldering with anticipation.

When she answered, her voice was unrecognisably thick. 'What'll happen if we don't answer the door?'

Clearly he wasn't keen to hit 'pause' either. Without releasing her forearm, he grabbed a corner of ocean-blue doona in his other hand and, with a decisive action, flicked it back. 'They'll get the hint.'

In a dreamy haze, she helped release his dress shirt buttons, then peeled the fabric from his broad, steamy back. As it dropped to the floor he embraced her again, somehow managing to manoeuvre her back and onto the mattress as he made love with his mouth and his hands. Quaking inside, she let her eyelids flutter shut. She felt almost desperate—in a way *starving* to know every mouthwatering inch of him. As he settled down beside her and his undiluted power radiated out, she knew that wish would soon be granted.

After he softly broke their kiss to sit on the edge of the bed, she heard his shoes 'thunk-thunk' onto the carpet. Tipping onto her side, she briefly wondered if he considered her shape 'puddingy' or curvaceous, but she buried the thought and cupped her head in a palm, ready to savour the fascinating vision unfolding before her.

His tanned, toned abdomen rippled and flexed as he slid off his trousers, then his shorts. Then he swung a crooked leg onto the bed and faced her. Awed by the complete bared-all package, she dared a two-finger stroke of his thigh—a surface that compared with sun-warmed granite. Cooper Smith had the body of a male swimwear model—tight, polished, bulging in all the right places. And that included south of the border.

Her mind was stuck on glorious freeze-frame when he urged her onto her back and, reclining beside her, smiled down, as if pleased by her level of interest. He held her hand and placed it on his sternum. Her more romantic side was convinced he had imprinted her touch on his heart.

The sound of his pleasure rumbled beneath her palm, deep and seductive. 'Your turn.'

Ready to return his smile, Sophie instead found herself holding her breath. All at once the shadow on his strong jaw seemed darker, the blaze in his eyes more intense.

No! She'd promised herself she wouldn't change her mind. But now the former, far more anxious Sophie whispered in her head. *Don't be a fool. You've bitten off more than you can chew.*

As if reading her thoughts, Cooper's smile vanished. Hair fallen over one side of his brow, he pushed up to support his weight on one arm as his gaze skimmed her lips, then examined her eyes. 'You're trembling.'

Sophie inhaled his fresh, earthy scent, drank in his concerned expression, and, suddenly feeling childish, shook her head. She wanted this. Would always remember it. All she had to do was take this last step. 'It's just that it all seems a little…surreal.'

The air compressed, then pulsed around them as he leaned in close to draw his bristled chin up her jaw. 'Great, isn't it?'

His reply was so gravelled and honest, so what she

felt as well, that Sophie laughed. Smiling again too, he rolled, sweeping her over on top of him with the movement. She went with the flow and, naked but for her panties, pushed upright to straddle his hips.

A moment of something like reverence passed between them before he reached around, held her behind and, his gaze lowering to caress her body, began to rotate his pelvis—back and forth, up and down. As she let herself go, closed her eyes and gently rocked above him, she felt his physical appreciation increase along with her own. Head lolling forward, then back, she worked with him—against him—till nothing barred their joining but crumbling restraint and an annoying strip of damp cotton brief.

Lost to the swirling depths of sensation, she was about to clear the obstruction when a hot fingertip began a tantalising ascent up her spine. Starting with circling at the base, his touch traced up over each vertebra—an action so subtle yet so exceptionally seductive it raised her skin to goosebumps and her soul to even dizzier heights.

By the time his touch arrived at her tingling nape Sophie's backbone had not only straightened, she'd over-arced. Her fingers dug behind her into his thighs, while her face worshipped those stars in her own private sky.

As she sizzled with need, he pivoted to a sitting position and, framing her face with his hands, kissed her so deeply she thought she might pass out. When he tried but failed to work a set of fingers through her coiffed hair, his husky murmur brushed warmth across her lips.

'I want it down.'

She smiled, blindly withdrew some hairpins, then shook out her waist-length hair. More freedom!

Teasing, she hitched up one shoulder and staged a pout. 'Ready for the wild Lady Godiva look?'

His brows opened up as he twirled one of too many curls. 'Wild is right.'

Her elation dipped. She combed a fall of spirals away from her cheek. She hated her hair. She only kept it long because it was impossible short. 'Is it *too* wild?'

'Absolutely feral.' He leaned in, dragged his teeth over her neck and growled, 'I love it.'

As exhilaration washed through her, his warm, wet mouth discovered the tender peak of her breast. She hummed with unabashed delight as his tongue worked its magic and the friction sparking low in her belly spread a marvellous liquid heat through the streams of her body. An arm bracing her back, he gently twirled her and lowered her upon the sheet.

The exquisite suction and occasional nip on her breast gradually eased. Sophie let out a long pleasure-filled sigh as his lips—his entire frame—began to travel down…over her lightly panting ribs, across her quivering tummy. The warm tip of his tongue trailed around and around her navel till she thought she might go mad.

Biting her lip, she pushed his head aside. 'That tickles!'

By the lamp's glow, she watched shadows move over the chiselled planes of his face. His eyes glittered with an authoritative style of mischief that left her weak all over. 'I'll have you know I'm being serious here.'

Oh, she believed him.

Her previous thoughts floated back, ribboning around the ecstasy of his mouth's moist caress as he angled closer to the juncture of her thighs. Inside, she held herself tight as the delectable ache of arousal grew stronger and deeper, until a fine spray of flaming arrows began to fly at her core. The intensity built to such a degree she barely knew she was writhing, or that her fingers were knotted in his hair. She could literally taste the ultimate satisfaction waiting a heartbeat away.

His slightly roughened palm skied down her waist, over her hip, till his touch delved past her panties' elastic and, curling beneath, met with the unmistakable evidence of her need. At the same moment she gasped at the contact, he snatched the scrap of fabric down and fully off her legs.

Bunched up inside, she shook like a kitten as he kissed her *there*, with such tenderness and obvious enjoyment that after a moment she forgot every concern other than being an aroused woman with urgent burning needs. She followed where he led, ever closer to the cliff, more than willing to freefall into the blazing whirlpool he had so effortlessly created within her.

Her climax crept up, then knocked her flying. An unfamiliar noise escaped her throat as she gripped his head and held on tight. The release was a continuous detonation of throbbing pleasure that kicked her hips off the bed and sent her soul soaring towards those far-flung stars.

She rode the rolling crest until the intensity gradually ebbed, and bit by bit she washed up on the shore. As the delicious ripples faded and real time began again, she dragged herself back and sighed on a smile. She needed to take a good deep breath.

Her eyes sprang open.

Oh, God, so must he!

Smothering a whimper, she released her hold. But when he peered up over the length of her body he didn't look concerned, or the least bit annoyed. In fact, he looked positively pleased as he prowled up on all fours, a sleek-muscled jungle cat stalking its second course.

A strong arm drew her near as, propped up on an elbow, his pure masculine perfection hovered close. 'Any regrets so far?'

Her heart squeezed.

Yes—but she wouldn't say it. She didn't want to even think it. This was the best she'd felt about herself in—well, since for ever. Her regret was that tonight would end; they would say goodbye. They were fundamentally different people, who thought and operated in very different ways. Cooper would find a beautiful agreeable woman who fitted his list, while Sophie Gruebella would carry on with her life.

The silver lining? Hers would be a *new* life, a metamorphosis, so to speak; tonight had proved that as nothing else could. From this time forward she made her own rules. The husk of 'pushover Sophie' would be left behind for ever. She couldn't wait to see Penny and Kate's reaction when she saw them next.

Cooper's voice was so low he sounded as dangerous as he looked. 'Miss Sophie Schoolteacher? That question requires an answer.'

Her lips curved as she twined her arms around the thick column of his hot damp neck. Thatching her fingers up through the back of his silky black hair, she shook her head. 'No regrets. No going back. Only forward.'

And, although her body buzzed with deep satisfaction, her sizzling nerve-endings already anticipated the next round. The best was yet to come. Three times, if she was lucky.

As he searched her eyes, his expression changed. 'You're beautiful.'

He said it simply, seemingly without artifice, and for a moment the breath caught in her throat. *But, come on...* She knew what lay behind that statement. Cooper might be alpha, and built, and sexy and rich. He also had a conscience. And right now that conscience told him to be kind to the girl he was about to know in the most intimate way possible.

She traced a fingertip around his cleft chin and lower, to circle his prominent Adam's apple. 'I know one thing,' she murmured.

A faint line brushed between his brows. 'Tell me.'

All warm inside, she tugged some chest hair and grinned. 'I'll remember this night.'

Returning her smile, he grazed the hard, ready length of his body against her. 'You won't need a memento?'

She pretended innocence. 'You could arrange one?'

'I do have something you might remember fondly. Unfortunately you can't take it with you when you go.'

He found her hand and redirected her attention…

The rest of the night and half the next day, Sophie enjoyed Cooper Smith's extraordinary hospitality. They didn't exchange addresses or any personal details. Exactly the way she wanted it. Him too. They'd agreed. They had no future together. This was one night and one night only. Neither needed to pretend to the other it was anything more.

Over the following weeks Sophie thought often of Cooper, but she tried never to dwell on his offhand suggestion of fond remembrances or mementoes. Until one Saturday morning when, alone in her apartment's bathroom, she gazed at the test stick and her jaw came unhinged.

Pink. Two lines. *Positive.*

In eight months' time she would be a parent.

Sophie crumpled back onto the pedestal seat.

And, like it or not, millionaire Mr Smith would be one too.

CHAPTER FOUR

COOPER scowled at the Roman numeral clock above his home office filing drawers and bit down as his stomach muscles clenched.

Eleven-twenty on a late autumn day. His surprise visitor would soon be here. Question was…what did Sophie want so many weeks after the event?

Frowning, he pushed out from his high-backed leather chair, rounded his desk, and absently rearranged a stack of depositions he should have finished assessing that morning. Instead, most of the time he'd merely stared at them in a slightly vexed, preoccupied daze.

The hotel had passed on her message asking him to call. Since their brief phone conversation yesterday, when she'd asked to meet with him here, he'd thought of little else. He loathed wasting time, but this morning he'd been dressed by six, had finished his workout by seven, after which he'd achieved nothing more than washing down endless cups of strong black coffee.

He glanced at the clock.

Eleven twenty-one. Nine minutes to go.

'Cooper, can you spare a few dollars?'

He jumped at the bright voice at his back, and the depositions scattered across the desk onto the floor. He spun to find his sister, dressed in worn low-slung jeans and a luminous pink midriff top. Her cropped blonde hair was styled to perfection. Shoulder propped against his office doorjamb, she munched on a bowl of rabbit food.

His arms folded over his chest. 'Is that what's going to fuel your day? A handful of lettuce?'

She was naturally small and lean, but a person needed sustenance—particularly when she was headed off in two weeks' time on a students' overseas exchange programme. The provincial city of Aurillac, France, was known for its chilly mornings. A little natural padding wouldn't go astray.

Paige arched a brow. 'And you've had...how many cups of coffee already today?'

He suppressed a grin. *Smart Alec.* 'We were talking about you.'

She mumbled something like 'bossy-boots', then issued a put-upon sigh and pushed off the jamb. 'Marlo and I will have lunch in between shopping, okay?'

His arms dropped to his sides. '*More* shopping?'

She stared at him, puzzled. 'Why else would I ask for money?'

He scrubbed at his jaw. 'Sometimes women's logic frightens me.'

'I need to upgrade my BlackBerry,' she explained, setting her china bowl on the sideboard. 'Treena Allen says mine is two whole models ago.'

He slid his wallet out from his back chinos pocket as he moved towards her. 'How much?'

'A debit card might be easier.'

He didn't flinch. 'No doubt it would.'

He handed one over, but she handed it straight back. 'Not this one.'

He grinned. No flies on Paige.

The card boomeranged back. 'It has a limit, Paige, but a very generous one. I'm sure you won't run into trouble.'

Knowing she was beaten, Paige succumbed to give a grateful smile. When she craned up, he bent down to accept a kiss on his cheek. 'Thanks, Coop.'

No big deal. Hell, if keeping his sister's techno needs in superior shape was the least of their concerns, he wouldn't grumble. When she started having trouble with boys, *then* he'd have something to say.

He blew out a long breath. God, he wished their parents were alive, then he wouldn't need to say things like this old favourite. 'No talking to strange men while you're out today.'

Paige groaned and rolled her eyes. 'Do we need to go through this every single time?'

While he had her attention, he'd slip in another one. 'And if anyone tries to pull you into their car, you scream and kick—'

'And run the other way. I know, Cooper. I know.'

She slotted the plastic into her designer handbag. 'I'm not a baby.'

He placed his hands on her small, vulnerable shoulders. 'You're my responsibility, and I take that responsibility seriously. You might not agree with what I say, but there's only one boss in this house. While you live under this roof I set the rules, and I expect those rules to be obeyed.' His voice lost some of its sternness. 'So, remember…home before dark.'

The doorbell chimed. Her expression alive again, Paige sprang around. 'I'll get it.'

Heartbeat slamming into overdrive, Cooper strode past. 'That's for me.'

Paige sideswiped his arm as she skipped past and overtook him. Naturally he couldn't let that offence go unchallenged, and he stepped on the gas. Paige crashed against the timber as they both skidded to a stop in the foyer.

Laughing, Cooper swung open the front door.

Sophie stood on the porch, wide-eyed and stiff.

He'd expected her to be glowing, like the last time he'd seen her. But in dark trousers, a white blouse buttoned to her throat and a black cardigan she looked staid and rather pale. Even her long tousled hair looked unfamiliar, tied back in a high, tight ponytail, though it was still super-sexy, with those haphazard spirals on either side.

But he wouldn't think along those lines. Sexy or not, no encore was permitted. They were as incompatible as oil and water—bedroom activities obviously excluded.

Paige wheeled in front of him and gasped. 'What are *you* doing here?'

Cooper squeezed his sister's shoulder. 'Paige, don't be rude.' No matter if she thought Sophie was a salesperson who'd ignored the sign at the entry gate. She needed her manners. 'This lady is here to see me.'

Paige squeaked at Sophie, 'You know my brother?'

Sophie's eyes shot wider. 'Cooper's your *brother*?'

Groaning, Paige smacked her forehead. 'Now it's coming together. Cooper must be the guy you've been getting all dressed up for.'

Sophie shrank into her collar and gave an awkward half-shrug. 'Who said I was getting dressed up for anyone?'

Paige laughed. 'It's kinda obvious. All the girls are saying so. It's like these past weeks you've had a makeover. New clothes, hair down—not like today,' she noted, inspecting the ponytail. 'Even the way you walk has changed. It's fantastic!'

Trying to track the conversation, and now hopelessly lost, Cooper held up his hands. 'Slow down. Someone fill me in on the missing piece of this puzzle.'

Paige spoke over her shoulder. 'Ms Gruebella is a teacher at Unity.'

Belated colour bloomed in Sophie's cheeks, but Cooper didn't allow his expression to let on either way. If a person had to hide a last name, Gruebella was one worth hiding.

And what about that second lot of information?
'You're Ms Gruebella from school?'

He'd imagined a fifty-year-old with wiry hair and
Victorian morals. Not a desirable goddess of a
woman with a voluptuous body, who had left him
sated and then instantly craving more. When he lay
down at night her unique vanilla scent flooded his
imagination. The vision of her reaching for him
gripped and didn't let go. Instead of their night fading, memories had become stronger, until when he
closed his eyes to sleep she was all that he saw.

But he needed only to recall those qualities which
could not and would not be ignored for sanity to return. Argumentative, ambivalent about marriage and
having children. And let's not forget her impulsive
nature. Of course he took full responsibility for
making the first move…the second and third, as well.
However, the fact remained she'd fallen into bed with
him in record time. Outstanding mistress material?
Absolutely. But he wanted a wife, dammit. Not sex
on the side.

He half wished he'd known the drawbacks before
asking her to dance. He could have saved himself
some sleepless nights, as well as what promised to be
an awkward meeting today if she planned on breaking
their agreement and seeing him again. As much as his
body might sit up and respond, this time he would
listen to common sense and years of field experience.
He had enjoyed their time together, but the answer to
any future liaisons would be a resounding *no*.

He knew best, and this was best for all.

A late model black Mercedes glided up and around the paved circular drive lined with soaring pencil pines. Paige's friend, Marlo Daniels, popped her head out of the lowering back window. Her large freckled nose scrunched. 'Is that you, Ms Gruebella?'

Paige wrung her handbag and addressed Sophie. 'You're not here over anything we've talked about, are you?'

Unease looped in Cooper's gut. He swung a furrowed glance between the two. 'And just what have you two been discussing?'

Sophie's face softened and she touched Paige's arm. 'I'm here to see Cooper about something else entirely.'

Paige seemed to think it through before she smiled, her teeth straight and white. Those braces had been worth every dime.

'Okay. But be good.' In a running skip, Paige headed off towards Marlo. 'Don't do anything I wouldn't do.'

As the passenger door closed and the Merc, Mrs Daniels driving, eased off, Cooper swept an arm through the air, ushering his guest in. Damn, she looked hot—

He set his jaw.

But not too hot to resist. When he made a plan he stuck to it. No detours.

Sophie edged in across the threshold. 'Small world, big school. There are quite a few Smiths. I didn't put it together.'

He brushed it off. 'Totally understandable.'

But her visit today had nothing to do with her being Paige's teacher—although he was grateful to have heard only stellar compliments regarding the mysterious Ms Gruebella. It made his impaired judgement that night seem slightly less unreasonable.

Passing a cosy sitting room, he automatically cupped her elbow. Even through her shirt's fabric, the powerful physical response sent lit fuses hopscotching across his nerve-endings. The impulse to linger and enjoy the sensation was crushing.

Inhaling deeply, he let go of her arm and slid his hand into his pocket. Small talk needed to be dispensed with.

He walked in step beside her. 'So, Sophie, keeping well?'

She swept her heavy ponytail over a shoulder and her gaze connected with his. Ah, yes, he remembered those eyes.

'Pretty much,' she replied. 'What about you?'

He shrugged. 'Trying to keep out of trouble.'

Without a hint of warning, her legs went out from under her. Whipping that hand from its pocket, he wove, and caught her weight as she buckled.

Finding her feet again, with his help, she patted down her hair and nodded at the marble tiles. 'Must be a slippery spot.'

He assessed first the floor and then his guest through narrowed eyes. They started off again. 'I'll have my housekeeper look into it.'

He opened a door that led off to a secluded patio—

his favourite place in the grounds, enclosed by mock-orange shrubs, with a goldfish pond to one side. Cooper often came out here to breathe in the unpolluted air, ingest the clear blue sky, and revitalise his sense of order and control. He needed a double dose today.

Stepping out onto the slate, Sophie trailed finger-tips along the border of bright green leaves before she lowered herself onto the calico-padded wrought-iron seat he'd retracted.

After dragging in his own chair, Cooper got down to business. 'When I received your message from the hotel asking me to call you, frankly, I was surprised.'

She avoided his gaze. 'I hadn't planned on calling.'

He waited. Cocked his head. 'Then why did you?'

He hadn't changed his agenda; he was looking for long-term. Sophie might have been too sweet to leave hanging on the vine, but he had a goal, and sampling her fruit again did not feature. She'd known that as much as he had.

Uncomfortable, she shifted in her chair. 'It's a little difficult to explain.'

Was she waiting for him to make the first move? Suggest they should pick up where they'd left off? It wouldn't happen. He wasn't buying. No matter how much her curls taunted him, or how much those plump lips he'd kissed till dawn tempted him.

In fact, the sooner this was out, the sooner she would leave—and the sooner they could both get on with their lives.

Of necessity, he injected a grave note into his

voice. 'I thought we agreed that night that we have different agendas.'

Hands clasped in her lap, still avoiding his eyes, she nodded deeply. 'Yes. Yes, we did.'

Cooper studied her more closely. Was this evasive, almost shy woman the same fireball who had detonated waves of heat through his blood? She still breathed flames over his skin merely by sitting near, clasping and unclasping the delicate hands that had travelled and aroused every inch of him. She was arousing him even now *without* touching him.

Brow low, knuckles knocking on the armrest, Cooper tossed an aggravated glance around. This setting was too personal. Too convenient. A more public environment would work best. No car blocked his drive so he assumed she'd taken a cab. They should have a civil discussion somewhere neutral, settle up and square off before he dropped her home. Case closed.

He tipped forward. 'This is a little awkward. I think we should go somewhere else for—' He'd almost said for coffee. But there was no forgetting what had happened last time he'd suggested that.

Finally finding his gaze, she filled in the blank. 'Go somewhere for lunch? I *am* a little hungry. I missed breakfast this morning.'

His thoughts jumped to Paige and her rabbit food, then his own stomach growled.

Her smile spread. 'Sounds like you did, too.'

His mind hurtled back to 'the morning after', when she'd taken great pleasure helping him devour chocolate syrup pancakes. They'd been naked, camped out on the rumpled sheets. He hadn't meant to drip the chocolate sauce on her thigh, though he sure as hell had enjoyed licking it off.

Slanting forward too, she clenched her white-knuckled hands atop the round table. 'But, Cooper, I really need to speak with you first. I'm not sure I can wait a minute more.'

He battled to keep the vision of her unclothed curves from his head. Not easy. But do-able. He was in control.

She sucked down a breath, but shot it back out on a nervous laugh. 'This is the hardest thing I've ever had to say.'

Her haunted expression...the note of concern in her voice...

The walls of Cooper's stomach gripped and he slowly frowned.

Was something more at work here than their night together? Was this somehow about Paige after all, and Sophie was reluctant to tell him? Was Paige failing a subject? She'd been struggling with maths, but he'd helped her out. She'd got a B last term.

Paige spoke of Ms Gruebella as a confidante.

Oh, hell.

He forced his mouth to work. 'Is Paige in trouble?'

Another statistic? A teenage pregnancy?

Sophie chewed her full bottom lip, looking at him from beneath her thick black lashes. 'Paige isn't in trouble, Cooper. We are.'

Cooper hadn't finished expelling a huge sigh of

relief before he registered the final part of her answer. A cog turned and he frowned. 'What did you say?'

Sophie wrung her hands on the tabletop. 'You know how we didn't leave the bedroom very much that night…or the next morning?'

Except to go to the couch and the spa bath. There had been that brief time in the pantry, too… He didn't quite recall how that had happened. Hell, they'd been all over the shop.

She went on. 'They say condoms are between eighty-five and ninety-seven per cent effective.'

And they'd used a few.

He formed the words to describe the bizarre notion in his mind. 'We're pregnant?'

She held up some fingers and a thumb to count. 'Due in seven months.'

He tried to take it in. His heart was throbbing in his throat. Echoing in his ears. Impossible to believe. This wasn't in his plan.

She groaned. 'I know what you're thinking. You don't want this complication.'

Complication?

Complication!

She wriggled straighter, truly meeting his eyes for the first time. 'But I've worked it all out. I would never have kept the news from you, but I won't bother you unnecessarily. You can see the baby whenever you want.'

The other side of the equation popped into mind and he tamped down whirling, exploding disbelief enough to ask, 'Are you fine with being a mother?' Last time they'd spoken she'd hadn't seemed sure.

'It was a shock at first.' A small smile played at the corners of her mouth. 'But, yes, I want this baby very much.'

Well, that had to be good news.

A line grew between her brows. 'I know you'll find someone, and soon, who'll be accepting about this. It's not the nineteenth century, where we'd keep this kind of situation locked up in a back closet. I'll get on with my life, you get on with yours, and I'll make sure the baby and I don't interfere with your plans.'

He ran a hand through his hair.

Get on with his life? Find someone? As in a wife?

His mind slid left and right like a vehicle skidding on black ice. He needed to get it all straight in his head.

This woman was having his baby. In seven months he would be a father. His child needed its father— not part-time but one hundred per cent. Needed a fully committed mother and father, both. If he knew nothing else, from raising Paige alone he knew that.

The blood drained from his head as he gazed at Sophie—beautiful, sexy, out-for-an-argument, life-is-about-luck Sophie.

His vision blurred and sweat broke out on his brow, down his back.

What the hell could he do? He couldn't marry her. He couldn't *not* marry her either.

Her voice reached him through the haze. 'It's a lot to take in, I know. But I've looked into it. I'll take maternity leave. And wonderful childminding options are available for when I go back to work, so it'll just be a matter of getting settled into a routine.'

He eased out a breath as the news started to sink in. Regaining some balance and strength, he waved a hand. 'No need for that. You won't have to work.' She'd stay at home with the baby. His baby. Their baby.

'Thank you,' she said softly. 'I knew you'd want to help out financially. But I *want* to go back to work. I won't give up teaching. It'll be an adjustment—sure.' One palm settled over her flat stomach as she smiled. 'But we'll be fine.'

Cooper grimaced at the queasy feeling in his gut. One half of him wanted to punch the air with excitement. He'd created a little human being—a son or daughter. After the recent demise of a two-year relationship, he'd harboured niggling doubts that was even possible. But it seemed his ex-girl-friend Evangeline Xiau had been proved wrong. He didn't fire blanks. Their inability to conceive must have been *her* issue—which was almost divine justice, given he hadn't a clue that Evangeline had been trying to fall pregnant until the day she broke it off.

Yet while the man in him rejoiced now, the lawyer wanted to know how he'd escaped one potential trap only to fall into another.

He shook his head at the ground.

He only had himself to blame. He'd had his fun. Enjoyed every moment. No use crying over spilt... Well, no use crying. Fact was he needed to marry a woman who was bound to drive him nuts. He must find a way to make the marriage work. Nothing mattered more. Because no child of his would ever grow up in a single-parent home. His child would not become a statistic.

Reaching across the table, he clasped her hand as a lifeless smile clung to the corners of his mouth. 'You're right. We're going to be fine.'

Clearly relieved, she exhaled. 'I thought you might hit the roof. You seemed so black and white about things. So needing to be in control...' She let it go and smiled. 'So, now that's out and settled, let's get that bite to eat. I'm thinking pasta Carbonara with warm crusty bread and chocolate fudge ice cream. Two helpings.'

He'd heard stories about pregnant women. They were known for erratic mood swings as well as cravings. Hormones on top of stubbornness and sparring.

He could hardly wait.

But he'd made his bed. He would be lying in it for a long time to come. He needed to focus on the pluses.

He'd wanted a family. *Check*.

More than instinct said Sophie would make a good mother. *Check*.

Paige liked her. *Check*.

An idea faded up through the fog clouding his mind. If he kept her busy and satisfied in the bedroom, where they got along best, she might lose the urge to be so objectionable. Happy wife, happy life.

But, first things first. Some arrangements needed to be made.

'After lunch we'll visit some jewellery stores.'

Her brow pinched. 'You've lost me.'

'When two people get engaged, Sophie, they need to choose a ring.'

Eyes wide, she shot to her feet. He pushed up too.

'Engaged?' she asked.

Was it truly such a shock? She must have known he'd pop the question. There was little else an honourable man *could* do.

'Cooper, I think you're forgetting something.'

He racked his brains—and then, understanding, took her hands and signed away the rest of his life. 'Sophie, will you marry me?'

She laughed. 'Absolutely not.'

Time stood still as he examined her wry expression. He clasped her hands tighter. He was in no mood for her games. This was serious—as serious as it got.

His words were measured, and not to be refused. 'Of course you'll marry me. You're carrying my child.' He would claim and hold on to it, no matter what it took. They would say their vows, become parents soon after, and everyone would be happy, dammit!

She looked at him as if he'd turned an interesting shade of green. 'If you've forgotten your list, *I* haven't. We won't work together. We both agreed.'

He re-anchored his weight. 'This changes things.'

'How?'

'We have the baby to consider now.'

'I *am* thinking of the baby.'

Alternate waves of heat and ice swept over his flesh. 'This isn't funny, Sophie.'

'Am I laughing?'

He found a placating tone. 'I'll grant you this is far from ideal. But surely you want your child to have a father.'

'He will have a father. I just won't have a husband.'

Teeth clenched, he examined the ground and rubbed his forehead. He was a strategist. He needed a strategy. Winning card first up: something they both agreed upon.

He moved in closer. 'Stop to consider the obvious benefits.' He lowered his voice to a sexy growl. 'Have you forgotten how compatible we are in bed?'

She coughed on a dry laugh. 'And suddenly sex is supposed to fix things?'

Well, it didn't make things any worse!

Next. He stood up tall—six-three, last time he'd been measured. 'I can provide well for the both of you.'

'You can do that without tying any knots.'

This had gone on long enough. He set his fists low on his hips. 'I'm not arguing with you. This is non-negotiable.'

She shook her head, bemused. 'It's started already.'

He held off from rolling his eyes. *Here we go.* 'What's started?'

'Having your boundaries and opinions and decisions forced upon me. I have my own mind, Cooper. I have my own dreams. And they've never included saying yes to a loveless marriage.'

That last sentence echoed his deeper conviction entirely—but they no longer had the luxury of dreams. 'We need to make this work for the baby's sake.'

'It would be a mistake to even try.'

He would convince her. He would make her see. 'I'll make it work.'

'Just like my parents thought it would work for them?'

His patience warped and creaked. Heart pounding against his ribs, he tried to keep his voice even. 'What about your parents?'

'My father and mother only married because they were having me. My dad was determined to do the right thing. My mother hadn't meant to get pregnant but, seeing she was, she decided my father was it. But they weren't in love, and love certainly didn't grow.' She pivoted away towards the mock-orange bushes. 'As far back as I can remember I've been the mediator. I thought if I found the right guy and lived happily ever after, somehow I could make their mistake half-right.'

His throat swelled. His parents had cherished both him and Paige. 'I'm sure they don't think of you as a mistake.'

She slid him a look. 'I'm talking about them getting hitched for the sake of their child.'

He rolled a shoulder back. 'What if they'd married and been happy?'

Her grin said she was unconvinced. 'What if we just agree to disagree?'

Not an option. He needed time to work on her. Some leverage. Anything.

A lightbulb went off in his head. 'I have another idea.'

'Does it involve food? Because that's the only one I've liked so far.'

'We'll have a trial run.' Until, that was, he convinced her to be sensible.

Her slim nostrils flared. 'You're crazy if you think I'd get married simply to see if we should divorce.'

No, no.

Seeing a light at the end of the tunnel, he ran his hands down her arms. 'I'm talking about living together.'

He read her eyes, the subtle change in body language at his touch. She was considering it.

But eventually she waved her hands and stepped back. 'Not interested.'

He shoved his hands in his pockets to stop himself from shaking her. 'Just for one moment can you stop being difficult? Surely you want to give our baby a chance at having a conventional family.'

Her green eyes glistened. 'People can start out with the best intentions. Doesn't mean there's a rainbow on the other side. You know that.'

Right. He'd go for the jugular. 'Think of it as an

experience. Let's say a three-month experience that could make a difference to the person you love most…your child.'

She stared at him for a long, torn moment.

'Three months?'

She was cracking. Good. And, if by some miracle she'd forgotten how their sexual chemistry sizzled, now he would fully remind her.

He drew her near, and the desire they'd shared before plumed in the pit of his stomach. His heart began to beat another rhythm as he remembered the way her limbs had felt twined around him, how she'd murmured his name over and over after he'd tipped her over the edge. He needed her to remember too, to convince her to do this his way. The only way.

Pulling her in by her shoulders, he didn't kiss her, but rather drank in the lines of her face with his gaze—smooth skin, kissable lips, eyes he still wanted to drown in. He couldn't see that ever changing.

Gradually the tension bracing her body eased. She didn't return his embrace, but neither did she push him away. 'Cooper, where on your list is love?'

His blood stopped flowing before he assured her, 'As of today I have a new list.'

Her mouth twisted to one side. 'If that's supposed to make me feel any better, it doesn't.'

'Then let's try this.'

With great purpose he lowered his head and kissed her, with equal measures of tenderness and meaning. A shower of electric impulses zapped over his skin.

Down below, his blood began to stir and heat. For a moment he was back in that room with Sophie in his arms and tomorrow a million light years away.

He needn't worry about luck. If the way her body quivered and pressed against him now was anything to go by, he had more than enough ammunition to succeed.

Because failure was not an option. He wasn't accustomed to losing, and before long Sophie would learn to accept that.

CHAPTER FIVE

SOPHIE was still reeling when she and Cooper arrived at the restaurant half an hour later.

On one level she took in the rustic brick front, with its green, white and red flag flapping from a mast, the mouthwatering aroma of freshly baked bread and tasty Italian herbs. But on a far deeper plane she was still experiencing that bone-melting kiss, his will wrapping around and attempting to crush hers in the most pleasurable way possible.

She was having this man's baby. Consequently he was determined to marry her. She couldn't think of anything more thrilling—or more self-destructive.

At the restaurant's entrance, a young male *maître d'*, dressed all in black, moved forward. With a broad smile, he nodded in welcome. 'Would you prefer a table inside or out today?'

Cooper said, 'Out', at the same time she said, 'In.'

Sophie shot Cooper an incredulous look. 'That southerly wind is icy.'

Evaluating the sky and the rustling sidewalk trees, he inhaled deeply. 'It's refreshing.'

Sophie studied the grey clouds churning overhead. Hunching her shoulders, she clutched each side of her cardigan and wrapped it more securely around her.

Cooper served her one of the persuasive looks she remembered so well. 'They have the patio heaters going.' He ran a finger down her arm. 'If that's not enough, I could keep you warm.'

Her body screamed at her to say yes, to give in. For so long she'd quietly dreamed of him overwhelming her with his unique brand of passion, as he'd done back in his garden when they'd kissed. But she meant what she'd said.

Cooper was indeed dangerous. If she was to keep her pledge to remain strong and assertive, rather than endlessly compliant, he was precisely the kind of dominant proud male she must avoid. A little late now, granted, but damage control was still available. She would not fall for his smooth talk and smoother ways, then submit to marriage.

In this day and age women had options and opportunities. No one needed to tie themselves to a loveless marriage for security's sake or anything else. Her baby would do better living alone with her than growing up in a house with two parents who couldn't agree on what day it was. She simply wouldn't put her child through the same ordeal she'd endured long ago. She would never forget how she'd tried to shut her ears to the quarrels that had risen up the stairs late at night, when her parents had thought she was asleep.

So why was she even considering Cooper's suggestion of a three-month trial?

A cold breeze blasted her face. She addressed the *maître d'*. 'Inside table, thank you.'

The young man hesitated, but when Cooper nodded, he collected two menus from a lectern and showed them through the wooden beamed archway into an area that exuded an authentic old-world charm.

A casual dark timber bar occupied the far corner of the low-ceilinged cosy room. Fresh flowers adorned settings dressed with green and red chequered tablecloths. But the ochre back wall caught her eye. It was dedicated to family photographs— black and white formal shots that might have dated back to the turn of last century, as well as recent colour snaps.

She knew the advantages of being an only child— no sharing bedrooms or televisions or parents. But at times it could also be lonely. What would it be like to grow up in a large, boisterous family? Like the one celebrating a toddler's birthday in the photograph that took pride of place in the centre of that wall. They all looked so happy.

Sophie thanked the *maître d'* as he retracted her carved wooden chair. Settling in, she set down her bag and, hands on the table, absently played with her bracelet's three-leaf clover charm.

After Cooper had removed his jacket, he shunted

in his chair. The light reflected off one of Sophie's charms and hit his eyes. He blinked down at her wrist. 'Who gave you the lucky bracelet? A favourite kooky aunt?'

Sophie bristled at 'kooky'.

She leant back as the *maître d'* laid a napkin on her lap. 'I bought it myself, just before the wedding.'

With a self-satisfied grin, he reached for the water carafe and filled her glass. 'And you haven't taken it off since?'

Oh, yeah. He was confident all right.

She lifted her water. 'Actually, the clasp is stuck.'

The carafe hovered a moment before he filled his own glass. 'I see.'

Carafe back in place, Cooper waved away the *maître d'*'s effort to place his napkin, then collected his leatherbound menu and fanned himself several times as he took in his surrounds. When his attention dropped to focus on the listed appetisers, Sophie rearranged the curls blown around her face by the breeze, pulled her cardigan closer, and found her own menu.

Although her first-trimester tummy was growling for nourishment, she couldn't concentrate on food. This pregnancy would change her and Cooper's lives for ever, but it would also affect Cooper's sister—who happened to be one of Sophie's best students.

She set the menu aside. 'How do you think Paige will react when she hears the news?'

But she could answer her own question: with great interest, no doubt.

When Paige had first broached the subject of sex and her boyfriend one day after English class, Sophie had advised she speak with her mother. After the options had been whittled down to no one being at home other than an overly protective big brother, Sophie had recommended the school counsellor. But Paige had been adamant; she trusted no one with her confidence but her favourite teacher.

Cooper had already flipped the menu over to peruse the dessert and coffee choices. His lazy gaze flicked up to stroke her. 'I've only heard her speak in glowing terms of Ms Gruebella. Seems you have fans everywhere.'

Even as Sophie melted at his suggestive look, she shuddered. How that title grated outside of school. 'What say we go back to pretending I don't have a last name?'

Cooper's approving nod seemed to convey a deeper meaning, and for the first time Sophie wondered about her first and his last names.

Sophie Smith?

Sophie bit her lip at the absurd impulse to find a pen and sample that signature on the napkin folded upon Cooper's bread plate. That urge hadn't been fully pushed aside before another question blinked in her mind. Her stomach dipped.

Whose surname would their baby bear?

Cooper set down his menu. 'Paige will most likely throw a party when she hears she's soon to be an aunt. She's always loved babies.'

Sophie knew that well enough. Paige had often said how much she wanted one of her own one day. Hopefully a big dose of babysitting would satisfy the yearning for a few years yet. Plenty of time.

Sophie paused.

Over the years she'd often wondered when or if she'd get the chance to be a mother. It was still difficult to believe it was happening now...this way.

Elbows on the tabletop, Cooper thatched his hands and brought them to his chin. 'So...what was Paige so concerned about you telling me?'

Thank heaven he couldn't read minds. She zipped her lips. 'Privileged information—sorry.'

'Teacher and student? Similar to sinner and priest?'

'Possibly more sacred.'

He broke eye contact to call the waiter over. 'Paige wouldn't be the young girl you mentioned had a boy hounding her?'

Sophie willed the hothouses from her cheeks and lied as she laughed at the suggestion. 'No.'

She trusted Paige to consider all the ramifications of taking 'the next big step'. After all, Cooper's sister was sixteen going on seventeen—a naturally curious young woman, not a tot. Still, Sophie was thankful Paige would be away overseas for a couple of months. Seeing how big the world truly was might help put into perspective the adolescent fires of love.

Which brought to mind her and Cooper's flames.

They hadn't discussed what intimacies would be involved should she agree to a trial. Sex or no sex?

That was a doozy of a question. Did living together include sleeping together?

In her mind she relived the captivating hours they'd spent enjoying each other, and a familiar warm compression kicked off a delicious pulse low and deep inside. The simple truth was, she wanted to experience those thrills again—what sane woman wouldn't? But if she allowed Cooper to make love to her, he wouldn't hesitate to use that power to manipulate her. Their kiss today had almost knocked her senseless. What defence would she have against him if a kiss turned into a night, a week, or *months* of mind-blowing sex?

She crossed her legs. As much as she adored the idea of getting naked with Cooper again, it simply was not wise. She'd feel continually drugged. In zero time she wouldn't know what the heck she was agreeing to.

A trial wouldn't make a fig of difference to how they fundamentally felt about each other. He would still be insufferably autocratic, and she would continue to tell him so—which in turn would make him more insufferable. But if she should decide to live three months under his roof—if only to prove irreversibly that his marriage suggestion was madness— she would need to keep both her head together and her clothes firmly on.

Best get that straight now.

She filled her lungs. 'Cooper, I was thinking—'

The muffled sound of a cellphone rang out.

Cooper held up a finger, found the phone on his belt and inspected the screen. 'I need to get this. Excuse me.'

Resigned, Sophie sat back. 'Of course.'

The *maître d'* showed up again. 'The gentleman and yourself are our only patrons as yet. Are you warm enough? Would you like the fire lit?'

Sophie sized up Cooper—head down, finger in his ear. She smiled over. 'A fire would be lovely.'

As the *maître d'* breezed off, Cooper disconnected. 'Did I miss anything?'

She eased off her cardigan. 'Nothing important.'

He settled the phone on the table. He nodded. 'I'm all ears.'

'Just for argument's sake, say I *do* agree to a trial live-in.' She ignored the assured gleam in his eye. 'We'd need to work out sleeping arrange—'

The phone buzzed and vibrated. Cooper peeked at the screen. He thumbed the answer button. 'Do you mind?'

Sophie lifted her chin to the phone and outwardly acquiesced. 'Go ahead.'

Was this a taste of what life with Cooper would be like? Dynamic men were busy men, oftentimes with lonely wives. Wendy was already finding that out. Noah had cut short their honeymoon in Singapore due to urgent business. Wendy said she understood; when a woman was married to a diligent and successful businessman, she more or less had to.

Cooper disconnected. His eyes roamed over her. 'You were saying?'

About to answer, Sophie held back as his gaze drifted over her shoulder and his brows buckled with enquiring surprise. His smile, a moment later, was close to reverent. 'Look who the cat's dragged in.'

Wondering, Sophie swung around in her seat. Her heart jack-knifed to her throat as a rush of disbelief and panic hurtled through her nervous system.

'What's *she* doing here?' she hissed, spinning back. Her eyes narrowed. 'Did you set this up?'

He kept his attention on the new arrival. 'No, but I wish I had. This is going to be fun.'

Pushing back his chair, he stood to address pretty Penny Newly, who had spotted them from the entrance. Finger and thumb to his temple, Cooper feigned a poor memory.

'Do we know each other?' He snapped his fingers. 'Of course. The wedding.' He spoke to Sophie. 'You know each other, don't you, sweetheart?'

Sophie's felt each corner of herself fold in on the other. This was an important, never to be repeated moment in her life, in which Penny Newly and her tactless remarks could play no part. She could throttle Mr Theatrical for instigating an encore to their exit that night.

But, to be fair, she couldn't snub Penny in this barely populated condensed setting. Perhaps taking the advantage and facing her insecurities head-on wasn't such a bad idea.

Finding her new, less mousy self, Sophie rotated towards her sometimes friend.

'Penny!' she exclaimed. 'I didn't know you visited this side of town.'

Her expression a study in curiosity, Penny glided over. She smelled great. Looked great. That white designer dress looked sensational against her spray tan and glossy, ash-blonde, perfectly ironed mane.

Penny barely acknowledged Sophie before offering her hand to Cooper. An admiring smile graced her full lips. 'I remember your departure very well, but I don't believe we've actually met.'

Cooper accepted Penny's hand. 'Time we did.'

Sophie held her breath.

Don't you dare say too much.

'Cooper Smith.' He gazed down at Sophie. 'Sophie and I were just about to enjoy a leisurely lunch. We missed breakfast.' His grin exuded charm. 'You know how it is.'

Penny arched a brow and considered Sophie. A beat too late she laughed, as if she understood perfectly. 'You met for the first time at the wedding?'

Cooper leant in to Penny. 'Do you believe in fate?'

Penny's perfect bosom rose and fell as he held her with his best bedroom-eyes gaze. 'I think so…yes,' she said, a little breathlessly.

'So do I.' He looked at Sophie with adoring eyes and she rolled hers. What a ham. He winked just for her, then spoke to the attentive Penny. 'Care to join us?'

Penny chewed her lip, as if considering, but shook

her head. 'I'm meeting someone. But we can catch up at my party next month.'

She slid a considering look Sophie's way. Sophie grinned. Penny's pink lip-liner was too dark.

'I'm sure I put your invitation in the mail...' Penny said.

What would the newly released Sophie say? She pretended to think. 'You might have. Can't remember if I've seen it.'

But Penny's attention had skipped back to Cooper. She all but gushed. 'No problem. I'll drop off another.'

Cooper tipped his head. 'I look forward to seeing you there.'

As Penny moved off, slim hips swaying, Cooper grinned across at Sophie. 'That should set the tongues wagging.'

'I'm surprised you didn't swoop me up and twirl me around your head on one hand.'

He reclaimed his seat. 'If only I'd thought sooner.'

She tried to frown, but secretly she'd enjoyed the show. Cooper certainly had a serious concrete side, but he could be the best fun, too.

His warm hand folded over hers, and a tingling flash sped up her limbs. 'Now, talk to me.'

The deep rumble of his words turned that tingling into a potent effervescent swirl that reached and then burrowed into her core. She battled to maintain an ambivalent expression. It would be safer to retract her hand. And she would...in just a minute.

'I was saying that if I agree to the three-month thing...'

He nodded. Moved closer.

She shivered at his intoxicating proximity and sucked down a breath. 'No sex will be involved.'

His brow dropped and he searched her eyes. 'Is there some problem? A complication?'

'Not the kind you're thinking. The baby would be fine.' Nodding, he moved closer still. She hurried on. 'I want you to know I don't believe our living together will change my mind that marriage is any kind of option. If we were any other couple you'd agree this is a hopeless cause.'

He dismissed her with a flick of his free hand. 'No need to go into that. Point is you're giving us the chance our baby deserves.' His thumb grazed the back of her hand and the smouldering swirl in her stomach spiralled lower. 'To give us the very best chance there can be no question. Sex is in.'

Her insides squeezed with longing, but she whipped her hand away. Face flushed with telltale heat, she shook her head. 'I won't back down on this. Making love will only muddy the issue.'

'The issue being whether we can make a decent, happy home for our child.'

Her heart thumped low in her chest. When he said it like that...

Her hands clenched into fists on her lap. Hell, he was a lawyer—a master manipulator. If anyone knew how to work a topic, Cooper did. But she was up to the challenge. A lawyer might think he was omnipotent, but a teacher possessed the power to shape the future.

Recovering her bearings, she shored up her line of defence. 'You're just trying to confuse me.'

He undid a cuff and folded his sleeve up the strong bronzed column of one forearm. 'Think about it,' he said in a deep, tolerant tone. 'We're practically strangers, yet bonded in an irreversible way. Clearly we need to get to know each other better. What better way than to pick up where we left off...where we got along best?'

Gradually she realised she was still looking at his arm, remembering how it had felt to have him tug her close and do exactly what he wanted with her, precisely the way she wanted him to.

As her breasts swelled with awareness and their tips hardened and rubbed, she snapped back to reality. To argue now would do more harm than good. She simply had to remember that, and never allow any hazardous situations to escalate out of control. There were such things as locks on bedroom doors, after all.

Close to okay with that scenario, she laid out her other provisos. 'Paige is leaving for her trip to France in two weeks. Yesterday after class she asked if I would go to the airport to see her off. That would be a good time to start our "living together" clock. But no contact with each other till then.' She added in an undertone, 'I have a lot to organise and get my mind around.'

His mouth slanted in a triumphant smile. 'Agreed.' He leant forward to seal their arrangement with a kiss.

She inserted a hand between their mouths. 'Did you miss the part where we haven't agreed on the intimacy issue yet?'

He captured her hand and eased it aside. 'Kiss me—it might jog my memory.'

Before she could find another barrier, he gently cupped her nape and pulled her close. His lips grazed over hers, lingering long enough for her heartbeat to hammer and her resolve to slip. When his mouth parted, and the warm, wet tip of his tongue touched hers, she somehow found the wherewithal to break away.

She tried to tamp down the mesmerising heat drifting through her bloodstream. 'Never forget that I'm doing this against my better judgement.'

He flicked out his napkin and laid it in his lap. 'Thank God your better judgement is wrong.'

CHAPTER SIX

Two weeks later, Sophie smiled into Paige's wide crystal-blue eyes and held tight to the teenager's finely boned hands. 'Don't look so worried. We're only a phone call away.'

Paige swallowed, then spoke over the noisy international airport bustle. 'I don't think I've ever been more excited or frightened in my whole life.'

More appealingly masculine than ever, big brother Cooper stepped into their circle. 'Two months in France will be an adventure you'll never forget.'

Sophie dragged her gaze away from the strong planes of Cooper's face to Paige, who was dressed in soft blue jeans and a comfortable yellow jersey knit for the long flight to Paris. She looked younger and more vulnerable than Sophie had ever seen her. Weird, but she even smelled like baby powder—although Sophie knew darn well Paige only wore fashionable fragrances, like the majority of seniors at Unity.

Hormones. They were playing havoc with her mind and her body. Her breasts had already jumped from a C to a D, and suddenly everywhere she went she saw people pushing prams.

Cooper cupped Paige's shoulder. 'If you have any problems with your host family, you know Madame Laurent will sort it out in no time.'

Sophie added, 'You must feel good, knowing your French teacher is chaperoning?'

When other duties allowed, Sophie and Madame sometimes lunched together in the staffroom. To avoid questions or awkward moments today, she'd let Madame Laurent know in advance that she and Paige's brother were on the verge of dating. Sophie had been a little anxious about letting the cat out of the bag, but Madame had seemed delighted.

Of course lifting the lid on her pregnancy would be something else again, and it seemed people were already talking.

Paige chewed her lip. 'It'll go quickly, right?'

With a fond glimmer in his eye, Cooper grazed a knuckle down his sister's cheek. 'We've travelled abroad before. Believe me, those weeks will fly.'

Sophie considered Paige's hands nested in hers, then relaxed slightly against Cooper's palm, which had come to rest low on her back. She had to concentrate to stop her eyes from drifting shut, the immediate heat of arousal was so intense.

As agreed, she and Cooper hadn't seen each other over the previous fourteen days. This morning, when he'd collected her from her apartment, as arranged via a phone conversation the previous week, the overwhelming sense of attraction and temptation had been so strong she'd imagined seeing sparks fly when they'd accidentally touched.

However, although the warmth infusing her body now was mostly due to serious sexual chemistry, the other reason for her pleasure buzz was the feeling of being included in this family—a feeling she could no doubt get used to alarmingly fast.

From a group of parents and their soon to be departed girls, Madame Laurent called over to Cooper. 'Mr Smith, could I see you before we go through?'

Cooper nodded, then assured Paige, 'I'll be right back.'

Paige eyed the gate she would soon pass through. She sighed so hard she visibly shuddered. 'I wouldn't feel so bad if I wasn't leaving Hallam for so long.'

Hallam Gregson: first-year university student, Paige's boyfriend, and, at her tender age of sixteen, the love of her young life.

Sophie put on a brave face. 'He'll be here when you get back.'

'I know you think it won't last,' Paige said earnestly, 'but Hallam and I really are in love. Like Romeo and Juliet.'

A shiver skated down Sophie's spine. They'd studied that Shakespearean play last term. Such a tragic ending.

Perhaps she should offer a suggestion. 'Maybe you could invite Hallam over for a Sunday barbecue when you get back?'

Paige had talked with the same passion about her secret boyfriend for months, but seeing her student out of school put a different spin on how Sophie interpreted the situation—and how involved she believed she should become. Time away from each other might defuse their feelings. However, if Paige felt this deeply when she returned, it might be time to introduce Hallam to the family.

Sophie smiled softly. 'I could even speak to Cooper beforehand, if you like. To lay a little groundwork.'

Paige blanched. 'Please don't do that. He'd freak. When Cooper found out I kissed a boy two years ago he went ballistic.'

Sophie could imagine. Still… 'I'm sure he'll understand that you're older now.'

Given Cooper was a lawyer who helped couples sort out messy family issues, and given how protective he was of his sister, no doubt he *would* react strongly to Paige branching out towards this next phase in life—dating. But putting on blinkers wouldn't make Paige's feelings go away, or stop her growing up.

Unconvinced, Paige shook her head. 'I'm not any older in his mind. He's great as far as big brothers are concerned, but he doesn't understand the first thing about how a girl thinks. His biggest motto is: I make the rules; you just have to follow them.'

Cooper reappeared, raking a hand through his clean, dark hair.

Each time she laid eyes on him Sophie felt her

heartbeat set off at a gallop, and a profound craving which had nothing to do with food gripped her stomach. She'd signed up for three whole months of this sweet torture, while making a vow never to succumb to his transparent plans for seduction. Refusing any and all invitations to his bed was the only way to arrive at a responsible decision regarding the possibility of matrimony. Unfortunately, as much as she couldn't see herself married to Cooper with his dominating nature, she could clearly see them making love. In fact, since their last meeting, that and their baby had been pretty much all she'd thought about.

Cooper spoke to Paige. 'They're ready to go through.'

Paige bounced up on tiptoe, kissed Sophie's cheek and whispered in her ear. 'Thanks for coming today—and for listening.'

While Sophie acknowledged a heart-warming rush of affection, Paige threw her arms around Cooper's waist. Kissing her blonde crown, Cooper hugged his sister back. 'Remember to eat a decent breakfast. And watch out for those French boys.'

Paige broke away. Eyes glistening like stars, she waved as she joined the other girls moving through the gate which led to the waiting lounge. 'I'll send you a postcard from the Louvre.'

Cooper waved back. *'Bon voyage!* Phone when you get there.'

Paige curved a hand around her mouth as she disappeared from view. 'I think you two look really cool together.'

With Paige gone, Sophie and Cooper each exhaled, then shared a look. Her gaze was drawn to the sexy curve of his lips as he grinned and said, 'Guess it's just you and me.'

As they set off down the wide, now less crowded thoroughfare, Sophie trembled inside. Tonight would be the first they would spend together. In Cooper's house. Alone. Like Paige, she was excited and yet scared to death.

She stepped onto a stretch of motorised walkway. Strolling alongside, Cooper took a few seconds to realise he'd lost his companion. As he stopped in his tracks, Sophie put on a sad face, waved goodbye, and let the walkway carry her further away.

Cooper's eyes flashed, before he pushed up his sleeves, took a running leap and scissor-jumped over the rail, landing just behind her.

Outrageously surprised, she laughed as he steadied himself, then squealed when he pulled her close and growled, 'Can't get rid of me that easily. I was regional high-jump champion three years running.'

His smiling mouth inches from hers, his hot, masculine scent wound out to envelop her, and for one crazy moment she almost succumbed to an overwhelming urge to wrap her arms around his neck and kiss him hard. Not a good start to her pledge to reject his charms.

Locking that impulse soundly away, she smoothed

back her curls and asked, in a remarkably steady voice, 'Have you done much travelling?'

He stepped back, but remained close, his broad chest almost brushing her shoulder. 'Some. What about you?'

'Not yet. But I've decided I really want to see the Eiffel Tower, the Statue of Liberty, Big Ben… I want to see it all.'

'Though you won't be jumping on a plane any time soon.' He laid a light hand on her tummy. 'Risk of premature labour.'

Sophie mulled it over. 'Isn't that only from the thirty-sixth week?' Molly Saunders, a teacher from Unity, had been pregnant last year, and had done the research.

Cooper's jaw jutted. His tone was low and adamant. 'Can't be too careful in your condition.'

When they stepped off the walkway, Cooper linked her arm through his. Given this kind of connection was a long way from kissing or, heaven forbid, making love, Sophie saved her energy and complaints, and instead quietly enjoyed the comforting sense of protection his strength offered.

Ten minutes later they were seated in his black soft-top. Cooper checked over his shoulder, slotted the gearstick into reverse, and backed out of the park. 'When do I meet your family? They'll want an introduction to the father of their grandchild.'

A cold wash of dread swept over Sophie's body. She clutched the tote bag on her lap and stared blindly out of the window. 'No rush. They're a couple of hours' drive from here.'

He stole a curious glance at her as he steered out into the traffic. 'We have to do it sometime.' Then he read between her tight-lipped lines. 'I'd be happy to be there when you break the news about the baby.'

Sophie predicted the scene—her mother unsure whether to be happy or devastated, her father torn between being proud and concerned.

She blew out a resigned breath. 'They'll probably jump on what they'll see as the obvious remedy and want a date set for the wedding.'

His left hand reached to claim hers. 'Soon we'll be able to give them one.'

For a heartbeat she thought about disengaging his hand and lopping it back on the steering wheel; she didn't like feeling crowded by his assumptions. Not one bit. Fortunately for him, she *did* like the way her toes curled in her boots and her blood sizzled at his touch.

But it wasn't enough.

She shivered beneath a shower of tingles when his thumb grazed back and forth over her fingers and he settled back into his seat as if they'd been driving together like this for years.

As if he'd won.

She grinned. She really had to admire such incredible confidence. Still… 'Don't get excited. I'm not even remotely close to agreeing to marry you. Just because you want this to happen, it doesn't mean it will.'

Wishing wasn't getting. Not even when a person was so obviously used to pursuing and attaining exactly what he wanted.

He flicked an unconcerned look into the rearview mirror. 'I disagree.'

She summed him up, so cool and invincible. 'Are all lawyers so arrogant?'

'Are all teachers this hard-headed?'

A rush of ridiculous disappointment fell through her. Alone barely fifteen minutes and the barbs were already out.

She slipped her hand from his. 'You sure know how to flatter a girl.'

His glance ran the entire length of her body. She gripped the seat. How did he do that? Set her alight with just a look.

'I meant want I said to Penny the other day,' he said. 'I believe in fate. We will marry because it's obviously meant to be. No use fighting it, either of us.'

She adjusted her seatbelt to turn slightly towards him. 'That's a line. You're not superstitious. You said you don't believe in luck.'

'Fate isn't superstition, and it has nothing to do with luck. It's science. What happens in our lives was always meant to be.'

She wanted to disagree, but she wasn't certain that she could.

He expanded. 'The relativity of time plus a sequenced order of events equals destiny. It's where planning and possibility collide. Admittedly this isn't how I envisaged finding my wife and starting my family, but here we are. I won't run from it. You shouldn't fight it.'

Sophie took in his summation and her heartbeat tripped. A delicate question that needed an honest answer knocked at her brain. That night when they'd stayed together Cooper had decided he was done wasting time, that he was ready to make a commitment.

She formed a string of words in her mind, then pushed out the first before she could swallow the whole lot back down. 'I have to ask…you didn't doctor any of the condoms, did you?'

He slid her a fractious look. 'You know the answer—but, no, of course not. In fact, I had absolutely no expectation of conceiving.' He switched on the radio, turned down the volume. 'It was fate.'

Hmm…

'Boy and girl having a good time. It happens. Sometimes even with contraception. We're living proof.'

'And sometimes it doesn't happen even when a couple tries for years.'

Sophie sat very still, waiting for the rest. She had a feeling it would be extremely revealing.

Cooper's brow furrowed, as if he were thinking it through. Then he indicated and veered off onto the shoulder of the expressway. With traffic zooming by, he shut off the ignition, laid an arm loosely over the back of her seat and spoke directly to her eyes.

'I was involved with a woman for two years. I

wasn't ready to settle down. She was. She thought if she fell pregnant it would hasten the process. She broke it off a few months ago because she wanted a family and didn't believe I was capable of giving her one.' A muscle ticked just above the square angle of his jaw. 'Although she'd led me to believe otherwise, she hadn't taken the contraceptive pill for over a year.'

Sophie's annoyed response shot out. 'She tried to fall pregnant without telling you?'

'Apparently her biological clock was ticking.'

When he shifted, his unbuttoned collar gaped wider, revealing a hint of the hair Sophie had ploughed her fingers through the night he'd made untiring, liberating love to her. Right or wrong, she didn't want to think of Cooper in another relationship. But it was his confession time. It would change nothing in their situation, but she would do him the courtesy of listening.

'Her cousin had gone through the IVF deal for years,' he continued. 'Evangeline saw how that affected her and her marriage, and decided to bail out of our barren relationship while she could.'

Sophie predicted how Cooper must have felt. Angry. Wounded. Worried. 'You thought you might have the same kind of delay with any partner?'

He shrugged a maybe. 'I didn't know which of us was responsible for the hitch, but I knew I wanted a family some day.' His eyes darkened. 'Sitting at that wedding reception, it suddenly seemed right to start looking for the future Mrs Smith.'

She gave a lame smile. 'And now the baby egg has come before the chicken, so to speak.'

He combed back the curls framing her cheek. 'I hardly think of you in those terms.'

The gesture tied her midsection in a flurry of loops. Perhaps she should take the roundabout compliment—but the truth was obvious, and had been from the moment she'd told him of her pregnancy and he'd proposed. He wanted to commit to her not because of who she was, but because of what she could give him—a gift that a part of him had doubted he might ever receive...a child of his own.

Cooper wanted to come home to his wife and baby every night. Was she his destiny? Or simply part of a pre-wrapped package?

The car's engine fired back to life and they drove in silence until, halfway home, he swerved off again—this time in front of an old-fashioned suburban grocery shop. He pulled on the handbrake and swung out of the car. 'Time to sweeten the mood.'

Still mulling over their conversation and her reflections, Sophie followed and sat outside the shop at one of two round plastic tables. When Cooper returned, her tastebuds burst to life; he held two monstrous double cones.

She clapped her hands. 'Triple choc. Just what I need.' She'd gone mad for ice cream since she'd fallen pregnant, and right now she definitely needed a sugar boost.

After he'd handed hers over, she got down to

business. She'd bitten off the lower pointed end of her cone before Cooper had even pulled in his rather rickety plastic chair.

He frowned as she munched. 'Don't bite the bottom off. It'll leak everywhere.'

She didn't bother explaining. Instead she grabbed his hand and bit the end off his cone too. She mumbled over the delicious cold and crunch, 'Die another day.'

She brought her mouth to the lowest opening of her own cone and sucked hard.

He fell back in his chair and chuckled. Then he shrugged. 'When in Rome…'

After striking the same elevated-cone pose, he latched on and drew the ice cream down into his mouth. He savoured the reward, swallowed, then licked his top lip.

'To think I'd have happily gone through life licking rather than sucking. In fact, we should explore that thought a little more.' He traced a suggestive fingertip up her arm. 'Ask not what you can do for your ice cream, but what your ice cream can do for—'

'Almost forgot.' Before his finger, or temptation, snaked any higher, she cut him off. 'Penny's invitation came in the mail today.'

Rocking to one side, she extracted a pink sheet of paper from her back pocket. The other slip of correspondence, which she'd also received that day, accidentally came out too.

Setting the principal's note aside, she lifted the invitation and put on a snooty voice. '"*You are invited to Penny Newly's Hollywood or Bust cocktail party.*"' She slapped the paper on the table. 'It's tomorrow night. What should we go as?'

'Depends on how daring you want to be.'

Conditioning, perhaps, but she couldn't think of anything bold. 'We could go as Clark Gable and Jean Harlow. But we'd have to do something drastic with your ears.' She thought about pulling the closest one out, wing-nut style. 'Or what about James Bond? And I could be the girl who holds your golden gun?'

Her cheeks bloomed. Had she truly said that?

Cooper's smile was pure sin. 'Consider that tabled for future discussion.' His attention dropped to the invitation and, next to that, the note. Frowning, he picked up the latter. 'What's this?'

Sophie thought about dismissing it, but it was a day for sharing. The first day of at least ninety.

'I received a message from the school principal today,' she told him. 'Seems he's heard some rumours.'

Cooper's brow dropped more. 'About us?'

'About the baby.' She shrugged at his questioning look. 'The only answer I came up with involves the principal's daughter—a student in my tenth grade English class. Dumb of me, but after they'd all left for final home class, I pulled out a baby's outfit I'd bought at the mall during my lunch break. I was smiling and hugging it to my belly when Samantha came back to get her sweater.'

He pushed the note back across the table. 'She passed her suspicions on to her father?'

'Actually, I think she told her friends. Then it was just a matter of time.'

'Now the principal wants a "please explain"?'

Trying to keep her anxiety levels down—being upset was not good for the baby—she studied the message. 'He can't terminate my employment. The days when teachers had to resign due to "personal circumstances" or marriage are long gone. But if he has a problem with single mothers teaching at Unity he might consider making my life there uncomfortable.'

'Uncomfortable enough for you to resign?'

She took a moment, then nodded.

Cooper's face hardened. 'I'll talk to him.'

She held up a hand. 'I'd rather you didn't.' Although his protective traits in this instance put a warm glow around her heart, Cooper's pride might only make matters worse. 'Anyway, I'm only surmising, thinking the worst.' She sat back. 'Might be he merely wants to let me know I have Unity's unconditional support, should I need it.'

Chocolate ice cream had drained over his fist. Cooper tossed the cone in a nearby bin. 'Either way, you can tell them as soon as tomorrow to keep their job.'

Sophie pitched her runny ice cream too. 'Why would I do that?'

'You don't need it.' He leaned forward, and she was hit anew by the searing force of his magnetism.

'When I said I'd look after you and the baby I'd never meant anything more in my life.'

Conviction shone from his eyes. One part of her couldn't help but be touched; another couldn't pretend to accept the offer.

She tried to disentangle herself from his overpowering allure. 'I told you… I like my job. I like the school.'

He wiped his fingers on the handkerchief he'd removed from his front chinos pocket. 'You'd like being a lady of leisure just as well.'

Her mid-section pulled. Was he listening at all?

She tried again. 'I worked hard through college. I love teaching and making a difference. A lot of my friends are teachers there. That's a huge part of my life, of who I am. I would never give it up.'

He consolidated his case. 'Only if the principal forces you to.'

Her heart smacked against her ribcage. She refused to feel cornered—by the principal or by Cooper. She had options. 'Then I'll get another teaching position.'

Cooper covered her chocolate-smeared fist with the handkerchief and gently wiped. 'We'll see.'

A jet of irritation shot through her. There was nothing to 'see'. She *wanted* to work. The last thing she needed was to feel indebted to him, or reliant upon his charity, and if she resigned that was precisely what she'd be: a commodity sponsored by Cooper Smith.

If she lost or gave up her job, and didn't find another, what would that do to their relationship's balance of power? Living in his house, surviving off his income... Would she then feel obliged to abide by his laws?

How had Paige summed up Cooper's thinking?

I make the rules, you just have to follow them.

Sophie understood Paige was a teenager—and he wanted to protect her—but did Cooper make any distinction between the two of them as far as that was concerned? Weeks ago she'd decided she would follow her own path, her own rules. She hadn't changed her mind, and, as much as he wanted to, Cooper wouldn't change it for her.

He squeezed her hand, determination shining like steel in his eyes. 'Understand that if and when you need me to step up and speak for us all, I'd like nothing better.'

Sophie understood very well.

That was what worried her.

CHAPTER SEVEN

'YOU ready?'

Cooper stepped back from Sophie's closed bedroom door and caught a glimpse of himself in the large teak-edged mirror at the end of his home's mezzanine floor hall. He frowned. Bare chest, longish scruffy wig, nothing left to the imagination about a pair of hairy muscular legs. Good thing the loincloth concealed the essentials.

Sophie's melodic voice drifted out. 'Did you say you'd picked out other costumes this morning, in case these didn't suit the party tonight?'

He was toying with the novel idea of thumping his expanded pecs when Sophie opened the door a crack. 'I'll need a big long coat,' she said. 'It's cold outside, and there's not a whole lot to this outfit.'

Her face looked fresh. Well, maybe flushed. Her eyes perhaps a touch more than alarmed.

His lungs deflated.

Jungle Fever had sounded ideal when the costume shop assistant had suggested it. Now, however, he wasn't completely sold on dragging his fists around in public dressed as Tarzan. All the same, he was eager to see how well his pretty mate had fleshed out her animal print.

As he drew closer, her vanilla scent tugged on his senses, and he found himself hurtling back in time. One word summed up that night perfectly: *sensational*. He planned for the next few weeks to be equally enjoyable.

Starting tonight.

He moved closer. 'Your friend will have central heating.' Beyond that, he would do his utmost to keep his Jane warm.

But Sophie hadn't heard. One set of fingers on the jamb, the other curled around the doorframe, her gaze drifted up and down the length of his body.

A glut of testosterone ran out to alert the team of this latest development. He puffed out his chest a little more.

She wolf-whistled. 'Don't know if my friends are ready for *that*.'

He found her hand and dragged her out. Jungle fever might work, after all.

Surrounded by spiralling dark ribbons of hair, her luminous green eyes stared out. Lower, a slash of *faux* fur fabric stretched over the ripe swell of her breasts; another adorned her curvaceous hips. Her still slender waist, slightly rounded midriff and shapely legs were left exposed. It was all he could do not to swing her over his shoulder like a sack and whisk her away to his treehouse.

Definitely later.

His bare toes wiggled against the carpet as she tossed back her head to shift a wayward curl hanging over one eye: a clear sign.

He accepted the invitation and reached out to play with her untamed mane. 'Jane silky soft.' His index finger trailed over her jaw. 'Want to throw some leaves around?'

'Only if they stick and cover some of our birthday suits,' she said. 'If I show up like this, I'll send everyone into fits.'

Physical need coursed through his system. Taking possession of her hips, he gently gyrated the lower strip of cloth as he surveyed the provocative picture before him. 'Do you have any idea how sexy you are?'

She quit squirming from his hold to peer up into his eyes. She looked maybe half convinced. 'I am?'

His thumbs pressed the sensitive dips either side of her navel and his pulse began to boom. 'Penny Newly had better be decked out as Kermit the frog or her envy will show big time. In fact, I have a better idea.' Drawn like a magnet to a ready supply of molten steel, his hips edged closer. 'Let's have our own party.'

She assessed his eyes, the suggestive position of their bodies. Her breasts jostled and unintentionally teased as she wrangled to disengage herself and return to the room.

Cooper's arms swung down, but the grin didn't

leave his face. She'd chosen the bedroom the greatest distance from his—as if that would keep them apart.

About to walk in and join her, he paused.

He hadn't thought till this moment, but a lot of stairs led up to this floor—a spiral of open timber boards. Well-positioned strips helped to grip shoes and feet. Nevertheless, the stairs needed to be approached, and descended, with care and respect.

He and Paige were used to them, but their once-a-week housekeeper had had a tumble recently. Thankfully, Joan hadn't been hurt, but neither was she pregnant. As he'd told Sophie yesterday, he would not take any chances with her condition.

Down the far end of the hall, the top of the handrail seemed to taunt him. Cooper considered again the possible dangers and nodded.

Tomorrow he would move Sophie's belongings into the guest wing downstairs. He would move into the adjoining suite. By the end of the week they'd be sharing one or the other.

He sauntered into the bedroom.

Standing before a white-lacquered dressing table, Sophie collected an amber bottle and spritzed her hair. When she saw his reflection in the mirror, the tassel on her teensy skirt arced out as she pivoted to face him. She tried to look in control, but the quiver of her bottom lip and saucer-wide eyes were dead giveaways. She wanted him to leave. More so, she wanted him to stay.

She placed a hand on her stomach and raised her

chin, defiant even in the face of defeat. 'I didn't invite you in.'

His attention dipped to the creamy length of her body—lines drawn by nature's brush on a very good day. He shrugged and closed the distance between them. 'Too late.'

When she took a step back, her animal print behind hit the edge of the table. She narrowed one eye at him. 'You're not going to start making monkey noises, are you?'

Stopping inches away, he loomed over her. 'I do feel rather primal.' He found her palm and rubbed it against his chest hair. 'What do you think?'

As her own chest rose and fell, he imagined the tips of her breasts tightening to the beads he loved to roll around his tongue. Sweet heaven, he could taste them now.

He was about to gather her in when she dodged around him. She stopped on a pastel-striped rug in the middle of the large room, her back to him, head lowered, hands fisted at her sides. 'I was surprised last night, my first night here, when you didn't try anything. You're making up for it now.'

Legs braced apart, he crossed his arms, enjoying her unease, her anguish, knowing it brought him closer to his goal. 'You had a big day yesterday. I wanted to give you time to settle in.'

Her reply was openly cynical. 'A whole twenty-four hours? How magnanimous.'

Arms lowering to his sides, he set off to join her.

'I might have considered giving you another day, but your costume has affected my thought patterns. I seem to have regressed back to using my primitive brain. I'm registering only two things.'

He ground into her back and let her feel what he meant.

Domination. Desire.

Jaw resting against her crown, he let his palms sail down her arms, ultimately securing her in place right where he needed her. These weeks had been an eternity without her in his bed.

He was about to taste the satin sweep of her shoulder when the purr in her throat turned into a growl. She broke away to face him, cheeks flushed pink, eyes dark with the same depth of passion that surged through his own veins. He felt the smile touch his eyes. This would be easier than he'd first thought.

'Cooper,' she begged, an ache in her voice. 'I can't think straight when you do that.'

He found a soothing tone. 'Let me do the thinking.'

Her hands shot up—stop signs. 'I do not intend to let you use those methods to persuade me to marry you. It's not fair.'

Sorry. Not a shred of guilt.

She must have seen that her pleas fell on deaf ears. Her voice squeaked as she backed up. 'We'll be late for the party.'

He grinned. 'What party?'

He'd told her this—*them*—was obviously meant to be. She might not be what he'd set out to find; he was not her ideal match. But damned if they couldn't make up for it in other ways. She couldn't argue with him if his mouth was covering hers.

Wary eyes stuck on his, she reversed up towards the opened door. 'This is crazy.' Her hand blindly found the handle. 'I've made a decision. These jungle outfits have to go.'

His hand went to his loincloth. 'All you had to do was ask.'

She jumped. 'No! I only meant this isn't going to work. We're going to that party, no matter what you say or think, but I'm not parading around close to naked in front of anyone—including you. I won't do it.'

When she practically stamped her foot, Cooper scrubbed his chin. Damn, she was stubborn.

He savoured the vision of his Jane one last time, then ripped the wig from his head and rough-housed his scalp. Best anyway. Aside from the animal instinct, he wasn't the Tarzan type.

He passed her and crossed out into the hall. 'You stay here. I'll get the other costumes. We'll change, go to the party, and get home to bed by a decent hour.'

She hid behind the frame. 'We? Bed? No, Cooper. This door has a lock, and I'm not afraid to use it.'

He smiled. As if that would keep him out.

But he'd feed her fantasy. In fact, a better strategy might be to withhold his affections. Give her time to realise just how much she wanted to revisit their night—again and again. She already knew his take on the situation: they should get to know each other more. Sharing a bed was the obvious place to start. Once he had her there, everything else would fall into place.

With that in mind, he constructed a suitable reply. 'I meant we should go to bed at a decent hour so you can get your rest. Perhaps we could get up early for a dip?' She'd seemed interested in the heated pool yesterday, when he'd shown her the grounds.

'How early is early?' she wanted to know, still on her toes. 'I'm on a timetable all week. Sunday's my day to sleep in.'

Ah, at last. Something they could agree on. 'How's eight sound?'

Her face pinched. 'I'm thinking more *late* morning.'

She unclasped the heavy beads hanging around her neck and they fell into her cleavage. His loincloth flexed, but he set his jaw. He'd decided slow and steady would win this race.

'I usually stay up late to watch the mysteries on cable Saturday night,' she explained, rescuing the beads from between her breasts—as if that action wouldn't aggravate a man in his condition.

Then he realised what she'd said. Mysteries were by no means his favourite. There were great alternatives. 'I prefer Union.'

'Civil war movies?'

He blinked at her. How did that connect? 'I mean football.'

Her expression didn't budge. 'You like football?'

'Most guys like football.'

'I'm not a guy.'

Obvious. So was her unimpressed state. Easily fixed. 'When you want to watch Agatha and I want to watch the Wallabies, there are plenty of televisions to go around. Two upstairs, three downstairs.'

She arched a brow. 'You watch a lot of TV?'

If he said he did, she'd only say she didn't. Watching television was the last thing on his mind.

He snatched a look at his wristwatch. 'Look at the time.'

She straightened. 'Leave the costume on the handle,' she said, closing the door, 'and I'll see you downstairs in five. I hate being late.'

CHAPTER EIGHT

'YOU'RE a late person, aren't you?'

Sophie frowned at the analogue clock on the dashboard as Cooper navigated the western suburb streets. Eight-forty-five. Penny's invitation had said seven.

She watched lamppost shadows chase over Cooper's classically chiselled profile as he replied. 'Only in so far as time is concerned.'

Sophie refrained from exhaling heavily. Late people drove her insane.

'Don't you have to meet with clients and be in court at specific times?' she asked. 'Surely you can't be late for appointments?'

'I compensate.'

'How? You make excuses? Buy gifts?'

He flicked her a got-it-covered look. 'I set my electronic reminder to go off thirty minutes before time. I also set my watch seven minutes early.'

Uh-huh.

'You don't get mixed up?'

He turned the wheel. 'Never.'

She thought about pointing out how crazy it all sounded, but if she had a right to be herself, she guessed he did too. This trial wasn't supposed to be about who was right or wrong, but rather the grey area in between—what worked as individuals as well as a couple. Not that she had any real faith that two people as different as they were could find enough space 'in between' to make a go of marriage.

Given their current highly sensitive states, wearing next to no clothes—particularly animal print— wouldn't work. Although feeling Cooper's loincloth pressed up against her hadn't been unpleasant. In fact, his fiery hands on her arms, his hot breath on her neck, had felt deliriously good.

So good she'd almost surrendered.

But if they became intimately involved again, she wouldn't be able to see the forest for the trees. He'd charm her into marriage and then, for better or worse, she'd be stuck. Divorce was an out, she supposed, but how would she fare in court? Cooper was a respected expert in divorce and custody issues. No. Best not to go there.

If they married, Cooper would still carry on with his life his way. No one and nothing could stop him. But she wanted to make her own choices too. Could she ever hope to do that married to a man like Cooper? She had intelligence and options. She didn't *need* to get married—and certainly not for convenience's sake.

A single-parent household wasn't the ideal, but their baby would be better off in that situation than with two parents who couldn't get along. Sophie needed only to remember her own childhood to be certain of that. How often had she wished her parents would admit that everyone's lives would benefit, not suffer, if they lived apart? They were *still* gritting their teeth, doing the 'right thing'—as if Auntie Louise and her father's friends at the bowling club *wouldn't* rather they separate and be happy individuals.

And if on Monday morning Mr Myers, the principal, suggested that wedding bells might save the school some embarrassment, then, as she'd told Cooper, she wouldn't waste her energies fighting but would rather find another job. Plenty of schools would happily hire a motivated and caring teacher who happened to believe she had a right to be a single mother too. Thank heaven most schools weren't stuck in the Dark Ages.

They found a parking space within walking distance from Penny's single-storey brick house. Cooper's thumb grazed a button on the steering wheel and the CD noise was shut off. Sophie eased out a breath. That particular blues collection was *so* not her favourite.

From the console, Cooper claimed the defining piece of his costume. He left the car and a moment later swung open her passenger side door. Before her stood Erik, super-sexy Phantom of the Opera.

After realigning his simple white mask, which

covered only half his face, he swirled and flicked his long black cape. His Transylvanian accent was impressive. 'How do I look?'

She grinned. She loved this lighter side of his personality.

She accepted his leather-gloved hand and eased out into the cool night air. 'Wrong horror movie. You're doing vampire central.'

He glossed a hand over his slicked-back hair. 'I thought at a pinch Mr Hyde…'

Cooper was no angel, but Sophie didn't want to think about him being *that* brutish.

She shook her head. 'Sorry. That voice is not Phantom, not Hyde. Definitely Dracula.'

Taken by surprise, she squealed when he tipped her back forty-five degrees. His nose rested one side of hers. 'That could fit in nicely with my new sucking preference.'

His fresh-mint breath and the rumble in his chest almost undid her, but she wouldn't let him know her bones had already begun to dissolve and she'd like nothing better than to feel his teeth dance over her skin.

Light-headed, she managed to push out a rebuke. 'Put the fangs away, Drac-boy.'

With a flourish, he swept her back onto her feet. 'You're no fun tonight, Christine. That costume is misleading.'

She smoothed the nineteenth-century replica peignoir which covered her corset and white stock-

ings. Her hairstyle hadn't changed from Jane's—
long, curly, loose.

He looped her arm through his and, bathed in the
golden glow of the full moon hanging in the Southern
Cross sky, meandered up the sidewalk.

He checked his watch. 'A couple of hours should
wrap this up.'

She started. 'We haven't even said hello yet!'

Jaw tight, he tampered with his cravat. 'I'm not
much for parties.'

Or was it that he was eager to get her back home?

However, Sophie could admit she wasn't much for
party small talk either. Nothing worse than those
long awkward pauses with someone you'd only just
met. Except when they stole a glance over your
shoulder to see who might rescue them.

However, that wouldn't be a problem tonight.
'These are my friends.'

'Hopefully not all as transparent as dear Penny.'

Sophie cringed. Would Cooper like her friends?
Nowadays she more often went out with her teacher
friends than anyone here tonight, but irrespective of
that…would Cooper be the kind of husband who
backed a girls' night out? Or would he turn into a
leave-'em-pregnant-and-barefoot type?

And what about that? Maybe he wanted a dozen
children? She hadn't thought past one. Not that they
were getting married. They were *not* getting married.
It was impossible.

Wasn't it?

Pocahontas—aka Penny—opened the door. On seeing Phantom, her face, between the long black braids, lit up. Her full lips slanted.

'*My* John Smith couldn't make it.' She acknowledged Sophie briefly. 'Mind if I borrow yours?'

'The name's *Cooper* Smith,' he reminded her politely.

'Cooper. Of course.' Penny's white moccasins and endless tanned legs made way as she gestured them through into her party-in-full-swing abode. Somewhere nearby a champagne cork popped and cheers went up. 'Care for a cup of my special punch, Cooper? It packs quite a—' She blushed. 'Well... punch.'

Cooper's smile managed to be both dazzling and thin. 'I'm sure Sophie would enjoy one too.'

Sophie didn't have to think this time. Purely for Penny's sake, she gave Cooper a private smile. 'We did work up quite a thirst this afternoon—didn't we, hon?'

Cooper's brows lifted. First in surprise, then in approval. He didn't need more encouragement.

Fooling with her peignoir's lacy neckline, he stage-whispered, 'Darling, you promised not to mention that once we got here.' Appropriately embarrassed, he turned to their hostess. 'Thank you, Penny. Punch would be great.' He touched his throat and rasped, 'I am rather dry.'

As they moved off, Penny prattled on about her house renovations. Cooper stopped and held a hand out to Sophie. 'Coming?'

The time seemed right for payback for crossing the loincloth line earlier tonight. 'You've so looked forward to catching up with Penny.' She blew a kiss. 'I'll see you both later.'

Above a knowing half-grin, his unmasked eye shot playful daggers as Penny dragged him and his billowing cape away.

Left alone, Sophie inhaled the aroma of the hot finger-food doing the rounds, then appraised the milling crowd—Terminator, Dorothy from Oz, Edward Scissorhands and, if she wasn't mistaken, Pamela Anderson, in a red one-piece that didn't come close to covering her famous bust.

Sophie rearranged her peignoir and smiled. Cooper was the kind of man most women dreamed about. Completely and irrevocably masculine. Confident to the point of arrogance. But Sophie didn't feel the least concerned that she would lose his attention tonight. Not because she considered herself more attractive or entertaining than any woman here, or because they were close to being in love. But rather because she was the mother of Cooper's unborn child, and right now that was all he could see. She would be a fool to think otherwise.

From behind, a set of hands swept over her eyes and Sophie jumped. She pulled them off and spun around to see Kate's razor-cut red hair hidden beneath a thirties-style blonde wig.

Kate circled her. 'Oh my God, Sophie—look at you!'

In a shredded dress and rope bracelets, Sophie was guessing Kate was King Kong's date, Fay Wray.

Kate's brow wrinkled. 'Have you lost weight?'

For once in her life Sophie felt wonderful saying, 'I've put a little on.'

Kate's gaze sharpened. 'What happened after Wendy's wedding? You didn't return any of my calls.' She craned a look around the busy, dimly lit room. 'Are you with that guy tonight?'

'As a matter of fact…' She buffed her nails.

Kate pressed a palm to her chest. 'I lost my breath when he carried you away like that.'

'Knocked me out too,' Sophie admitted.

That night had been one of a kind—overflowing with colour-filled magic. Every woman should be lucky enough to experience a night with a lover as expert as Cooper. Sophie's body flashed hot whenever she thought of the heights to which he'd taken her. Release had become more intense, more necessary, each time.

But would she enjoy those same kinds of thrills again? Though she would never admit it to him, she couldn't imagine being with anyone but Cooper.

Kate absently rearranged her ropes. 'I can't think why Evangeline cut him loose. I tried to dig a little, but she wouldn't give even a hint.'

Sophie's antennae picked up. 'You know Cooper's ex?' The woman who had tried but failed to conceive while they were an item…?

'Evangeline's a friend on Wendy's husband's side. Didn't come to the wedding for obvious reasons.' She mouthed, *'Too awkward,'* then nudged Sophie's ribs. 'Good thing for you, though.' She tilted her wavy blonde wig towards the kitchen. 'I saw her earlier. Guess she didn't realise her ex would be here.'

Someone nuzzled her neck from behind, and Sophie jumped, higher this time, then spun around.

Cooper, minus the mask, waved a cracker and spread under her nose. 'Chilli-cheese dip. I can get another.'

Spicy food upset her stomach—particularly now she was pregnant. She tried not to screw up her nose. 'You enjoy.'

He popped the cracker in his mouth, but stopped mid-chew as he stared off over her shoulder. His bright blue eyes doubled in size at the same time as his olive complexion came over all pasty. His voice was little more than a rasp.

'Evangeline?'

Nausea rolled up and down inside Sophie's tummy. Swallowing hard, she followed Cooper's eyeline while Fay Wray, obviously sensing hazards ahead, quietly slipped away.

A petite woman waved once, looked around, and, finding no escape, moved to join them.

When she came close, Sophie saw the woman's eyes were almond-shaped and deep hazel in colour. She smelled like roses—soft and subtle—and looked like an oriental princess—or was it geisha? She probably would even out of costume.

Her gentle tone was no surprise. 'Hello, Cooper. It's been a while.'

Cooper finished swallowing his cracker. 'Nice to see you.'

Madam Butterfly forced a smile. 'I didn't expect to see you here.'

A pulse leapt twice in his jaw. 'Small world.' He placed an arm around Sophie's corseted waist. 'I'd like you to meet Sophie.'

She could have kissed him for leaving off her last name.

Evangeline had the kind of face that reminded Sophie of angels—beautiful, serene. First impressions were everything, and although Sophie knew their background, she had a hard time believing this woman had taken matters into her own hands about starting a family with Cooper.

Sophie accepted her hand. 'Good to meet you.'

Cooper's gaze had dropped to Evangeline's waist. Seeing his frozen expression, Sophie stole a look too. She was no expert, but she'd place the gestational age of Evangeline's baby somewhere around six months.

A hot tingling flashed from the base of her skull all the way over to her beading forehead.

Oh, God…how long ago had Cooper said he and Evangeline had broken up? Surely this wasn't his baby too? Evangeline would have said something long before now.

Wouldn't she?

Cooper blinked rapidly at the half-egg shape under Evangeline's red silk dress. He coughed out a dull laugh. 'Got a pillow under there?'

'No pillow. I'm having a baby.' Evangeline bowed her head, cupped her belly and smiled. 'Actually, two. I'm having twins.'

Cooper pulled in his chin as if he were trying to digest the news. Or maybe he was counting backwards too. A fine sheen broke across his gelled back brow. 'That happened quickly.'

'Robert and I met the week after we broke up.' Evangeline shrugged an apology. 'Yes, it was very quick.'

Evangeline's unspoken words hung in the thick air.

It wasn't me who couldn't fall pregnant, Cooper. It was you.

After an awkward silence, in which the other woman held her stomach, Cooper knocked back his punch and Sophie withered in her shoes, Evangeline glanced over her shoulder.

'He's around somewhere. My fiancé,' she explained, looking back with a weak smile. 'You'll have to meet him.'

Cooper's smile was practised, but his eyes hinted that he'd been struck hard.

'Another time,' he said. 'We really ought to go.' He drew Sophie closer. 'Sophie needs her rest.'

Sophie did a double-take. Had she understood Cooper correctly? Had he just let his ex know that she was pregnant too? She hadn't even told her parents yet.

While Sophie got her bearings, Evangeline's fine eyebrows arched in astonishment, then delight. She looked as if she didn't know if it was safe to smile.

'That sounds like an announcement. Am I reading too much into that?'

Lifting his chin, Cooper eased back his caped shoulders. 'Triplets run in Sophie's family.'

Sophie almost spluttered. Then she almost slapped his face. How dare he use her like this. Divulge something so private and important merely to bolster his wounded sense of masculinity and show up his former girlfriend.

Ears burning with indignation, Sophie found Evangeline's eyes and pushed out through gritted teeth, 'We're keeping it quiet at the moment.'

Evangeline nodded her understanding even as she threw out her arms and drew Sophie in. 'I'm so happy for you both.' She stretched on silk slippered tiptoe to place a no-hard-feelings kiss on Cooper's cheek. Her eyes smiled her good wishes. 'Obviously I just wasn't the right one.'

Sophie and Cooper said their goodbyes and left five minutes later. Cooper was uncommonly quiet on the drive home. That was fine, because if Sophie had opened her mouth, she'd have torn him to shreds. Did he have any idea how it felt to have your feelings dismissed like that? He constantly told her he wanted this to work, yet how could it when Cooper's point of view and concerns were the only ones that counted? She was so upset with him she wanted to cry.

When they entered his house, Sophie began to stride off without a goodnight. But Cooper held her back with a gloved hand on her forearm.

She spun back to see him drag the cravat from around his throat. 'Tomorrow I'll move your things down to the guest room on this floor.'

Sophie studied the shadows in his usually clear blue eyes. Why did he want her to move? And what gave him the right to demand like that? She thrust back her shoulders. 'I'll stay where I am.'

'This is non-negotiable!' His expression cut from stone, he glanced up at the stairs spiralling towards the mezzanine floor. 'Those stairs are dangerous. I won't take any chances.'

Sophie's laugh was devoid of humour. 'Don't I get a say in what's dangerous and what's not? Don't I get a say in anything at all?' She wrenched her arm from his hold. 'How dare you tell your ex-lover that I'm pregnant?'

His gaze ran over her like a belligerent hot press. 'You can't hide from this situation for ever, Sophie. I have as much right to share the news as you do.'

'Without even consulting me first? That was nothing more than grandstanding at my expense.'

He looked down to rip off his gloves. 'We won't discuss it now.'

She knotted her arms over her waist. 'Now who's hiding from the situation?'

His gaze pierced hers, and the pulse in his jaw kicked off again. 'We were discussing where you'll sleep from now on.'

'How does my own bed at my own place sound?' She shook her head, tears of frustration filling her eyes. 'You've tried to push me around since I told you about the baby, but now you've gone too far.'

He moved forward till he towered over her. His voice lowered, more gravel than steel. 'I'll go as far as I need. Some things are too important for compromise, and my child's safety is one of them. You're staying here, and you're moving downstairs.'

Bully. 'No. I. Won't.'

Exhaling, he rushed a hand through his dark hair, then gave her a warning look. 'I won't argue with you, Sophie. In the morning you'll see that I'm right—about everything.'

He moved off towards an archway that led to the adjoining private theatre/TV room, but turned back to set a kiss on her forehead before disappearing.

Trembling, hating his kiss but wanting it too, Sophie let out a long exhausted breath. She knew he could be over-protective, domineering. But seeing Evangeline had brought those qualities out tenfold, and she knew the deepest reason why.

It wasn't me. It was you.

When she and Cooper had fallen pregnant so easily, he'd assumed that Evangeline's difficulty in conceiving must be hers. But with his ex falling pregnant as quickly as Sophie had, the question of fertility—and *infertility*—had been tossed into the air again.

Turning slowly, Sophie eyed the varnished timber, took several deep breaths, and then, lifting her peignoir skirt, ascended each stair carefully.

Cooper had made it clear he wanted a family more

than anything. It didn't take a mind-reader to know that now he must wonder...

Had the difficulty between he and Evangeline lain with him? Was this time—this baby—a fluke? No doubt he would get a specialist's opinion, but Sophie doubted he would get it next week.

Cooper had a light side, but ultimately he was a man who possessed determination. He'd funnel all his energies into making certain this baby was born safe and healthy. Incorporated into that objective would be his resolve to continue to keep this child under his watchful eye and protection.

From the top of the stairs, Sophie gazed down at the soft flicker of the television dancing across the timber floor below.

A part of her couldn't help but sympathise with Cooper. Tonight had been a shock. But, damn it all, even if he *did* have a point about the stairs, it didn't mean he had the right to bring down the law and expect her to jump.

Removing her drop earrings, she headed for her room.

Tonight she would let him unwind.

Tomorrow she needed to decide whether it was time to call this charade off.

CHAPTER NINE

SOPHIE woke the next morning feeling awful. She'd barely managed any sleep. Her mind had been a tumult of revolving conversations from the previous night. Most particularly those final moments with Cooper.

Dragging her feet, she showered, dressed in a baggy jumper and jeans, and for the hundredth time contemplated how best to handle the scene that would no doubt confront her this morning. She was not prepared to bow to Cooper's demands. She'd been crazy to accept this challenge in the first place. Never again would she be made to feel as if her opinion didn't count. As if *she* didn't count.

She opened her bedroom door, her heart physically aching. She would remain strong. This was over. Hell, it had been over before it began. And, no matter how much Cooper wanted to control the situation, there was nothing he could do to make her stay. She'd been here less than forty-eight hours, and already the shells were falling. This house would turn into a war zone if she stayed any longer. And what about her unborn child? Playing house and pretending things could be different were not conducive to maintaining a healthy pregnancy. The baby's well-being must come first.

Before she tracked Cooper down, she smelled pancakes—fresh, hot, baking now. The aroma, and her empty stomach, tugged her straight into the kitchen. By the hotplates set in a huge island bench stood Cooper, dressed in worn jeans, and an unbuttoned white shirt, and with bed hair that looked ten times sexier than his usual neat style.

In the middle of flipping a pancake, he must have sensed her there and glanced over. Their eyes met and his Adam's apple bobbed. 'Hi.'

Sophie swallowed hard. She'd had every intention of telling him this was over, that she was going now and calling a cab. How dared he pull this on her? How dared he look so vulnerable, yet more masculine than she'd ever seen him?

He nudged his bristled chin at the bottle of sauce on the counter. 'Chocolate,' he said. 'Hope you're hungry.'

A lump swelled in her throat. 'If this is supposed to be an apology, it won't work.' Hell, she almost meant it.

He left the pancake cooking and moved towards her, his gait fluid, his broad shoulders rolling. Her skin flashed hot and her stomach tied in one big aching knot when he didn't stop until his body touched hers and his large hands cupped her face. God, he smelled good. She'd take his musk over pancakes any day.

She shook herself back.

No! She had to leave before this overpowering attraction crushed her spirit totally.

She tried to weave away from him. The muscles in his arms and chest bunched and flexed as he held her firm. His skin was steamy, his exposed torso uncompromisingly hard.

He tipped her chin up to have her look into his eyes. 'I'm going to say something.'

She wanted to block her ears against the hypnotic rumble of his voice. 'We said all there is to say last night.' He'd embarrassed her, then ordered her to obey his demand that she sleep where he saw fit. Suffocating emotion burned her throat. 'I'm not a child, and I won't be treated like one—not by anyone, not for any reason.'

She almost saw it…the former Sophie waving goodbye and stepping back for ever. No matter how much she wanted Cooper to overwhelm and kiss her—and, yes, beg her to stay—she simply couldn't.

'I won't apologise,' he said, in the rich deep timbre that sent ripples lapping up her spine. 'Not about you moving downstairs. You don't want to hear it, but I'm right. If you slip and lose the baby you'd never forgive yourself, and I would never forgive myself for not protecting you both.'

Somewhere through his speech she'd stopped struggling. She hated to admit it… Could she admit it?

He was right.

Unshed tears stung behind her eyes. She wanted to

run away, hide. Wake up when everything was sorted and she and her baby could live happily ever after.

Her voice was a strangled whisper. 'You hurt me, Cooper.' Through telling Evangeline about the baby as much as anything.

His thick sooty lashes lowered as his hand combed back her hair. She felt his heartbeat booming through his body and against her. 'Forgive me.'

Her heart squeezed. *Oh, God.* Did he have to look at her like that?

'Tomorrow you'll be asking me to forgive you again.'

His jaw flinched as his gaze lowered to her lips. 'I'm not perfect.'

She hesitated, then somehow, somewhere, found a small grin. 'Can I get that in writing?'

The tension bracing his frame seemed to ease. He took half a step back to search her eyes more deeply. 'Does that mean you'll stay?'

He was insufferable, boorish.

Dangerously close to irresistible.

She set her jaw and tried to look fierce. 'It means you're on probation. That's your one and only Get Out of Jail Free card.'

As he groaned with relief, drew her in and pressed an almost chaste kiss to her brow, she didn't know if he realised, but in her heart she knew it was true. She owed it to her baby to give him one more chance. She owed it to herself and the baby to stick to that and not give in again.

CHAPTER TEN

ONE month and one day after the costume party, Sophie stood looking over the meerkats' replica desert home at Sydney's Taronga Park Zoo. No winding caves or upper storeys. These cute cousins to the mongoose lived on ground-floor quarters.

Just like her.

But she didn't regret giving in to Cooper's request that she move downstairs. It would be arrogance on her part to say she did. And, to be fair, after their talk-and-make-up that morning he'd been on his best behaviour. So much so, she'd begun to wonder whether miracles did happen and destiny had in fact shone its light on them both.

But it was early days yet. Surely a leopard didn't change its spots? A man of Cooper's determined and uncompromising character didn't turn over a new leaf overnight. Each day when they said goodnight, and she curled up in her bed alone, she told herself, *Wait a little longer and the bombshells will start falling again.*

Every day she waited for the former Cooper to return. Every day she waited for the sparring to begin again. And every day that passed without a sighting, she found herself believing and caring a little more.

Whistling, Cooper returned with two bottled waters. He set one upon the waist-high fence and, smiling at a meerkat's pointed little face and alert upright posture, unscrewed the other bottle and handed it over.

Sipping on her water, Sophie wondered again at Cooper's newfound restraint with regard to trying to seduce her. Was this self-discipline part of a calculated game to have her crumple beneath the incessant craving and beg him to take her in his arms?

If that were indeed the case, all she could say was… it was working. Whenever he smiled that certain sexy way, or strode around in front of her in nothing more than a towel and foam upon his face, she had to call her body to heel. Unfortunately it never listened.

After removing his baseball cap, Cooper swiped the bottle's condensation over his brow. The winter sky was a perfect dome of saturated blue, and the temperature had been delectable—though it was dropping now the afternoon was fading.

After quenching her thirst, she recapped her bottle, and Cooper turned for her to slot it into the khaki knapsack slung over his back. 'We should visit the kangaroo park next,' she said. The last stop on today's busy agenda.

She adored the clean, open atmosphere of Taronga Park. More so, she loved that endangered species like the Asian elephant and Nepal's Red Panda were being cared for here.

He checked the time. 'Then we'd better get a move on. They'll be closing soon.'

They meandered down a gently winding bitumen slope, Cooper keeping a half-step ahead—Sophie suspected in case she stumbled or tripped.

He snapped a digital pic of a massive croc grinning around a mouthful of jagged teeth. Showing her the shot, he asked, 'Any update from the infamous Mr Myers this week?'

Cooper was aware that, as it had turned out, the principal hadn't wanted to see her regarding anything personal, but rather had needed to discuss a parent's complaint over a student's assignment mark. Perhaps it was nerves, but Sophie had imagined a curious glint shining from behind Mr Myers's large old-fashioned frames as he'd spoken to her from his orderly desk that day almost a month ago.

'I must have been mistaken,' she said, stopping to read a direction chart to make sure they were on the right path. 'Myers still doesn't seem to know anything about the pregnancy.'

'But he'll need to soon.'

Irrespective of how well things had been going between them, her hackles quivered. They'd been through this. 'I don't want to hide it. I just don't feel a need to blurt it to the world.'

Her body. Her privacy. Her prerogative.

And there was another reason for not jumping in

and telling everyone at work—the first twelve weeks of pregnancy were known for incidents of miscarriage. But she had entered her second trimester, thank heaven, and was discovering a whole new interesting side to her fluctuating hormone journey.

Cooper seemed to read her mind.

'What were you looking up on the net last night? You shut the page when I came into the study.'

Sophie quashed a jab of embarrassment and twisted her mouth. 'Hmm…sorry.' She shrugged. 'Can't remember.'

He laughed—a deep, rich, scrumptious sound. 'You look as guilty now as you did then.' He gave her the evil eye. 'You weren't tinkering with the naughty sites, were you?'

She dug deep for an answer. 'Not exactly.' Then, more firmly, 'No.'

They collected a bag of dry food pellets and entered a reserve full of kangaroos and wallabies but, almost at closing time, devoid of humans. The minty smell of eucalypt was close to overpowering.

Opening a pellet bag, Cooper walked around her. 'I see you're trying your best to intrigue me.'

He followed as she trod carefully up to a grazing wallaby. Sophie crouched, and glowed inside when the sweet little face nuzzled into her hand. Their eyelashes were so long—she ran a palm down its back—and their fur so incredibly soft.

Cooper nudged again. 'Anything you want to share, Sophie? I'm all ears.'

The wallaby's wet nose wriggled against the pocket of her palm, full of pellets. She shrugged again. 'Just information about being pregnant.'

They stood back as a six-foot emu, Australia's flightless national bird, trotted by.

'I feel as though I'm pulling teeth.' Cooper stuffed his empty wrap into his back pocket. 'Will you tell me what you were researching, or do I get worried?'

She shook the rest of her bag's contents onto the ground, and two more wallabies edged over on their long tails and hind legs.

He wanted to know.

She inhaled deeply.

Okay. She would tell him.

'Fluctuating hormones.' She knew she ought to zip her lip now, but a force greater than common sense seemed to spur her on. 'Some women experience a phenomenon where their sex drive increases in the second trimester. Husbands sometimes complain they can't keep up.'

She stole a glance at Cooper.

His lopsided grin said, *I can keep up.*

Avoiding his eyes, she moved towards the smooth dimpled bark of a giant gum tree. 'It also says that this phenomenon might be linked to women's basic need for reassurance during this time.'

That's quite enough, Sophie.

After dusting his hands on his chambray button-down shirt, Cooper joined her.

Pressed against the trunk, hands fanned behind her

at the pit of her back, she still couldn't bring herself to meet his gaze. Not even when he stood close enough for that mesmerising innate heat to seep though her clothing, burrow through her skin, and find that secret place deep inside. The force was so tangible she pictured red and blue flames leaping to life.

They'd made love for an endless night and half a day. Had seen each other dressed in nothing but desire. Yet her cheeks burned with the blatant implication of her own words. Did she want to take them back?

Sophie's shoulders sagged. Foolish or not, she wanted the safety of his strong sinewy arms around her. The urge for contact had become so overpowering lately that twice this week vivid dreams had woken her...

Cooper's hard-muscled body above her.

Adoring lips nipping hers.

Hot male scent convincing her more and more.

His sable voice wove out to soothe her. 'If you can't say it, Sophie, I will.'

She closed her eyes and shivered as his warm breath stirred her hair and hot fingers threaded back the curls fallen over her face. He cupped her hip and scooped till he'd prised her away from the wood.

'We want each other,' he told her. 'We're not kids. Nothing is bad or wrong with feeling strong physical attraction towards a person you care about.'

Sophie's heartbeat skipped, then she smiled. He cared about her? As much as she'd come to care for him?

Cooper murmured against her crown. 'Here's something else to think about. What if we make love two or three more times and the sparks fizzle and die? Shouldn't we find out whether our physical attraction is long-term or just a flash in the pan?'

Sophie grinned. Oh, he was smooth. She had a big feeling her sparks for him would never fizzle.

Which sounded romantic, but in reality wasn't necessarily a good thing. If this trial failed—if she still believed he wanted to marry the chicken who had incubated his egg rather than the person he respected, valued and, yes, maybe even loved—she didn't want to be hung up on a lost cause all the lonely years of her life.

He brushed aside more stubborn curls on her brow. When he dotted a soft kiss on her hairline, her core squeezed with the unmistakable sweet pang of longing. Concentrating on the rapid rhythm of her heartbeat, she breathed in and out, then, forcing herself over caution's edge, walked her fingers up his shirtfront.

Thing was, he did have a valid point. Didn't he? Maybe they really ought to check out whether their compatibility in the bedroom was not only as real and wonderful as she remembered, but also whether it would last beyond a night…a week…a month…

His hand framed her face as his thumb worked a light, relaxing circle at her temple. 'We need to check those waters out thoroughly.' His mouth caressed the spot. 'Very thoroughly.' He groaned and held her closer. 'Very, very thoroughly.'

Her mouth drifted over and skimmed his. 'Cooper?'

'Yes, sweetheart?'

Sweetheart.

She smiled. 'I get the picture.'

Smiling back, he tasted her parted lips.

Her arms gradually linked around his neck, and he gathered her in for a passionate and meaningful no-holds-barred kiss.

A thunderbolt of searing heat fell through her middle and down her legs, before gushing back up in a fanfare of tingling bright lights. Hanging on tight, she invited him in fully, revelling in the fire that burned and leapt inside her. Time converged in on itself, a twirling, giddy spin that left her breathless, weak and needing more.

Needing it all.

When the kiss ended, Cooper's breathing was laboured, his voice thick. He nipped her bottom lip. 'We need to go home or the kangaroos are going to sell tickets.'

She floated up from her dreamy haze to see an audience of marsupials arced around them, eyes bright, apparently most eager to witness the next stage.

He found her gaze. 'I might not believe in black cats and lucky charms, but I do believe our night together wasn't a mistake. *This* isn't a mistake. I want you, Sophie.'

He stole another penetrating kiss that melted the last of her resistance before reluctantly drawing away.

His smile was soft. 'Let's go home.'

With the afternoon's cool shadows growing longer, and their arms looped around each other's belts as they left the reserve, Sophie so wanted to take heart in Cooper's confidence. But that annoying part of her which wasn't affected by raging hormones niggled and whispered all the way home.

Whether or not she'd been a party to it, ultimately Cooper had got his own way. As of tonight, his bed was her bed.

CHAPTER ELEVEN

'Drop the bathrobe—but only if you're naked underneath.'

Freshly emerged from a steamy shower after their big day at the zoo, Sophie enjoyed a delicious shiver at the authoritative tone evident in that deep, masculine voice. Sexual awareness climbed as, poised in the *en suite* bathroom's doorway, she allowed time for her eyes to adjust from the brighter light to the bedroom's corner lamp glow.

The commanding silhouette towering before her gradually acquired features. As Cooper's hooded gaze became clearer, so too did his hungry smile.

The plateau of his chest was dusted with the wiry hair she adored driving her fingers through; the toned ridges of his stomach looked as hard as her whispered memories said they would be. Hair began again below his concave navel, arrowing down in a silky trail that left her heart beating so fiercely she could barely catch her breath.

He pushed out a put-upon sigh and rushed a hand

through his damp, dark hair. 'Guess I have to do my own dirty work and come over there.'

Cooper moved towards her with the athletic grace of a predator savouring the thought of its next, highly anticipated meal. His rolling muscles were a masterpiece in polished steel motion. His Levi's were her favourites—well-worn, low-slung and unzipped. With each languid step the soft blue denim shifted on his hips, drawing her attention to what Sophie knew full well lay beneath.

Light-headedness tingled across her brain as the distance separating them narrowed and his scent reached out to fill her lungs. Finally anchoring his weight mere inches away, Cooper cuffed strong fingers into the collar of her heavy towelling robe and urged her up onto tiptoe at the same instant his mouth came crashing down.

Impatient, greedy…she happily submitted to the drugging magic of his kiss. The force was greater than any current catching her ankles and sweeping her out to sea. She was drawn in by the urgency, set free by the heady heights of passion. Some good reason had stopped her pursuing this intense longing these past weeks, but for the life of her now she couldn't think what.

Stretching, she moved to embrace him, but found her robe's shoulders had been dragged down, effectively confining her arms to her sides. Smiling against his lips, she burrowed close as his large hands continued to pull the towelling till her heavy breasts spilled out.

As his thumbs kneaded her arms, her nipples rubbed against his chest, releasing a scorching blast of want that struck and then consumed her feminine core. Legs turned to rubber, she clung to his forearms, willing this night to last at least until eternity.

As their kiss evolved into starved snatches, he urged her to follow as he backed up. His tongue was tickling a responsive patch on her neck when she imagined his legs hit the mattress, and something resembling conscious thought clawed its way up from the depths of wild abandon.

Still, it took the hot shell of his hand slipping under the robe for her to remember the all-important questions she'd decided, while showering, she needed to ask.

'Cooper,' she murmured, eyes closed, neck arced back, 'we need to stop for a moment.'

He manoeuvred her around till she sat on the bed's edge, then pressed her back against the dusky pink coverlet. His gaze trained on her swollen tender breasts, he released the tie at her waist. The hot plates of his palms ironed across her abdomen as he spread the robe apart.

In shadow, she saw a pulse jump at the side of his throat and one dark brow lift in shameless appreciation. 'Yep. You're naked under there, all right.'

His knees nudged hers apart, widening her thighs to a vee before a two-fingered touch slid a lazy path between her centre. As a powerful tremor gripped her, her hips automatically arched to meet his stroke.

Cooper's smile changed.

The side of his hand breezed down then up one quivering inner thigh. 'I've missed you.'

A knee on the bed, he lowered over her.

A flash went off in her mind. She remembered her preparation plan and rolled away.

Chuckling, he effortlessly rolled her back. 'Sophie, all the fun's happening here.'

She swallowed hard and gathered her thoughts. 'I need to ask you something. And I'm sure you'll say yes, because that's the answer any man would give, and that's what a woman would expect. But be warned. I'll see in your eyes whether or not you're telling the truth.'

He froze, before finally falling onto his side. 'This sounds more complicated than trigonometry.' He eased up onto an elbow and, cheek in hand, nodded. 'Go ahead.'

'It's really very simple,' she said, assembling her thoughts and tamping down, as best she could, the sizzling physical overload. 'Do you believe in monogamous relationships?'

One of Cooper's brows took on a curious slant. 'Sophie, have you developed your own list?'

She thought about it, and had to admit it. 'I guess I have.'

His lined expression eased considerably. 'In that case...' He twirled a fingertip around her closest nipple and she stifled a groan of pure pleasure. 'Yes, Sophie, I believe in one partner only.'

Predictable answer. Still, she took heart seeing the easy conviction shining from his eyes.

He grinned. 'Did I pass?'

She shook her head. 'Not yet.' Not needing any distraction, she pulled her robe closed.

'But I didn't fail.' He reopened the robe. 'So don't mete out the punishment just yet.'

Feeling exposed, but secretly revelling in his attention, she tried to ignore the allure of his devilish smile. 'I would never cheat on an exam, and I would only steal if a loved one's well-being was at stake and I had no other choice.'

He tipped his head, impressed. 'I not only like it, I agree.'

He angled across and oh-so-gently traced the tip of his tongue around that beaded, screaming peak.

Fighting down the urge to draw up her knees and haul him close, she pushed his head back. 'One more.' Her blood was on fire; she needed to hurry. 'If someone was drowning, and there was a danger I might drown too, I'd have to jump in regardless.'

'The courage versus stupidity conundrum?' He truly looked at her this time. 'We're on the same page there too. I'd do the same.' His eyes stayed with hers and he brought his arm over and kissed one corner of her mouth. 'Am I free to go, miss?'

Smiling, she framed his firm, square jaw in her hands. 'You are most certainly not free to go. You need to stay here and clean the boards…' he kissed the other corner of her mouth '…and put up the chairs…' he nipped her lower lip. She sighed. 'Then, and only then, can you make love to me till dawn.'

Grinning, he pushed away to stand at the foot of the bed, where the bathroom light set a hazy aura around his sublime Adonis shape. Sophie watched, entranced and shaking a little inside, as the jeans slid down the long firm trunks of his legs.

Cooper filled his lungs with softly scented air, kicked aside his jeans, and again joined the woman he was dying to enjoy.

All-consuming desire pumped through his veins as he threaded an arm around her waist and tipped her so they lay front to front. Every nerve-ending leading to his groin ignited as she curled into him, offering herself up to a pleasure they both knew would only increase as the hours fled by.

Funny. From the second she'd accepted their live-in arrangement he'd harboured plans to seduce her, whether openly or covertly. But there was nothing contrived about the way his heart boomed now, or this sense of belonging drifting through his bloodstream.

She'd accepted his decision about the stairs. Tonight she'd admitted that surrendering to their passion was inevitable. Soon she would understand that his resolve to marry her was also non-negotiable.

He respected Sophie and her desire to stand tall and be herself. He'd come to care deeply for her too, in ways that had sometimes left him aching and wondering where to funnel all that emotion. But tonight they'd found the answer: in each other's arms.

They hadn't had a disagreement in a month, and were alike in the matters that truly counted. Their morals, their sexual attraction towards each other. Their baby. Should anything else matter?

Her hand fluttered over his stomach and latched on to his most eager appendage.

'You haven't forgotten about my raging hormones, have you?' she purred. 'I might just run you ragged.'

Bone-melting comets shot from his crotch down to his toes and back up again. Don't worry about turning his dials. Already she was close to blowing him off the map.

He cupped her rump and shoved her roughly against him. 'Stamina, thy name is Smith.'

He hadn't finished the sentence before a bolt of shame tore through his centre and he realised what he'd done—manhandled her backside as if she were a piece of un-pregnant meat.

Had he caused damage? Should he shoot himself now?

As gently as his growing dread allowed, he moved back and examined her face, her belly. 'Are you all right?'

She looked at him as if his brain had been invaded by alien beings. 'I'm fine. Wonderful, in fact.'

'I didn't hurt you? Maybe hurt the baby?'

Her warm smile went a long way to soothing his charred conscience. 'The baby is protected, Cooper. Don't worry.'

He probed her eyes. 'There's nothing I can do that will harm him?'

'At this stage? Not a lot.' She coiled her leg provocatively over his hip. 'But if you need to find your sea legs, front to front is very safe.' Her teeth grazed his chin. 'Or so I've read.'

Happy hormones of the XY variety surged to wash away any remaining doubt. He held her raised thigh and eased her close against the length of his body. 'Your research?'

He dropped a kiss on her temple, her cheek, her soft, welcoming mouth.

'Mmm… Cooper…?'

His blood was liquid lava now. 'Yes, sweetheart?'

'Let's not talk anymore.'

He chuckled. 'I like the way you think.'

He *loved* the way she felt. Her skin smooth as satin, her hair bouncy and soft. Best of all he loved the way she gripped him when he finally entered her, bit by bit, holding back long enough to know she was ready, as she'd never been before.

They held each other, pressed in tight, his body damp with perspiration, hers slick with desire. Their synchronised rhythm continued to increase until the urgent push of anticipated reward couldn't be denied one moment more.

He felt her muscles tense at the same time as his

mind closed down, the dam broke loose, and he shuddered with the visceral joy of pulsating release.

He groaned and held her so close that some part of him was convinced they had morphed into one. He'd never felt more complete than at that moment. She was his again, and would be from this night forward. They belonged together, for so many reasons, and he would make certain nothing and no one ever tore them apart. What he had now, what he treasured most, he would never let go.

When the waves finally died, and the physical intensity ebbed away, he inhaled deeply and, running his palm up and down her smooth back, reflected on the thrill of making love again at last. And didn't it just beat all? In no time he was craving to know her again—with his arms, his mouth, with everything that made him a man.

He heard and felt the crinkle as she nuzzled her cheek against his chest, then sighed long and loud. 'Mmm, that was good.'

Smiling at the heat already stirring in his loins, he breathed in the sweet fragrance of her hair. 'If that was good, I can't wait for fantastic.'

Her tummy gave a quiet growl, and he frowned.

He didn't want to bust up the party, but he guessed they really ought to break for sustenance; she hadn't eaten since lunch, and that couldn't be good for the baby. Thirty minutes and they could regroup for a variation on tonight's 'safe sex' theme. He could barely wait.

He was about to suggest roast beef and homemade potato salad sandwiches, but stopped when she rubbed his cheek in a let's-lie-here-and-talk kind of way.

He held her a little tighter. 'Something up?' Besides the obvious.

She paused before taking a deep breath. 'What do you want more than anything?' She dropped a warm kiss at the base of his throat and looked up into his eyes.

He covered her hand with his, and in a solemn voice told her the truth. 'I want to keep this child, our child, safe and always under my care.'

She seemed to think it through. 'What does that mean, exactly? You want to give up your job to be a full-time caregiver?'

He chuckled. He loved her sense of humour. 'That's not exactly it, no.'

'Or is it that you want to come home each night,' she continued, 'knowing that your wife has cared for your baby and your house?'

He paused. He recognised that tone. This was one of her trick questions. The answer was an unreserved yes. But instinct said she wanted to hear no.

He wasn't going to jeopardise a month's good work and argue now.

He'd just let it slide.

But she persisted. 'What about childcare? Nannies versus larger facilities? Maybe you'd be prepared to work twenty hours a week instead of fifty or sixty, so you could do three days at home with the baby one week, two days the next?'

He frowned. Was she serious? 'Besides other considerations, at this stage in my career that's not feasible.'

'But you'd be happy enough for me to give up *my* career?'

Heartbeat thudding in his ears, he let go of her hand to rake his hair back from his brow. He stared at the ceiling. Clearly swinging her around would need some work. But not now. Plenty of time to discuss what was best for everyone over the coming days and weeks.

His hand found hers again, and this time he squeezed. 'We've just made love. I don't want to argue.'

'I'm not being argumentative. I'm addressing issues that need to be addressed, whether we marry or not.'

His jaw tightened. With the dividends from his investments, they would live on the sunnier side of easy street the rest of their lives. He understood she might want to hold on to part of her independence, but after the birth surely she'd want to spend the majority of her time with her own child rather than other people's?

She cut into his thoughts. 'I want to show you something.' Moving her hand from beneath his, she made a fist and presented him with an elevated view of the closed pinky end. 'See that line between the creases of my hand and curled little finger?'

He looked closer. No, but anyway…

'That indicates how many children I'll have,' she said. 'I have one line, which means one child.'

Oh, come on, now.

He slanted her hand away and sat up. 'I don't believe that old wives' tale, and neither do you.' She was angling for a reaction—a way to introduce her next point.

She covered herself with the robe and sat up too. 'What if I only want one child? What if I want my career, just like you do?'

There were bigger issues that might be better handled, say, a month from now, when he'd completely convinced her that they were getting married and living together with their child, no matter what.

'How many children would *you* like, Cooper? And don't you dare suggest triplets.'

Thoughts of Evangeline and her pregnancy popped into his head. Had their difficulty in conceiving been his or hers? Maybe neither. For some, conception occurred easily. Other couples endured long delays sometimes for no apparent reason. He'd learned recently that a fellow lawyer and his wife had tried for five years, given up, adopted a golden retriever and then last month—bingo! Would he and Sophie fall so easily a second time?

Sophie wanted an honest answer. He'd give her one. 'I'd like two children—a pigeon pair. But I'll focus on this one. If he is born healthy, I'll be happy.'

'But Cooper—'

Enough!

He tackled her with a silencing kiss. They fell back on the bed, and soon her resistance had melted into acceptance.

As the caress eased and their lips parted, Cooper was gripped by the almighty urge to say…

Something.

I love you?

No. Way too soon. And if he didn't believe it, neither would she.

But, looking down into those big green cat's eyes, he felt the heat begin to build again and the want become a need.

Was he falling in love for the first time? More importantly, was Sophie falling for *him*?

He curved his hand around her crown and slanted his mouth over hers again—neither too hard, nor too soft, but hopefully just right.

Because timing and skill were vital. When he had her heart without reservation—when she was in love with him and couldn't give up what they had together—then he would have what they all needed most.

His family—their family—safe and sound under one roof.

CHAPTER TWELVE

ONE month later, Paige was home from France, Cooper was still playing nice and Sophie had actually begun to think about diamond rings and white dresses. Not that Cooper was aware—and she wasn't about to tell him. Not yet. She still wasn't certain, but…

Maybe soon.

She was daydreaming about Cooper wrapping her in his arms and saying the three little words she longed for and needed to hear when the front door slammed shut. Her heart leaping to her throat, Sophie frowned and shot a look towards the kitchen wall clock. Five past five. Cooper was home early, and it didn't sound as if he'd had a good day.

Wiping her hands on a teatowel, Sophie tossed a harried glance over the vegetables she'd chopped for tonight's stir fry. Two months ago, when she'd first moved in, she wouldn't have believed she'd be standing here behind Cooper's kitchen sink playing wife. She still wasn't certain she believed it.

They were yet to work out the dinner thing. He liked big home-cooked meals. She liked to eat out. His housekeeper usually prepared three or four dishes that could be removed from the freezer when needed. But Joan was away, visiting her cousin in Ireland, so Sophie had taken a stab at 'big' and 'home-cooked'. Cooking itself didn't bother her, but she begrudged the time spent cleaning up afterward. Now Paige was home, she could help.

Sophie quashed the tug-of-war going on in her mind and collected her chopping knife.

All in all, cooking wasn't a huge deal. And Cooper got a laugh whenever he saw her in this old-fashioned apron.

Cooper strode into kitchen, his face dark, his bearing dangerous. Sophie held her breath. At times he could be focused, preoccupied, and he never completely lost that 'I know best; people need to listen' mentality. But she'd never seen him like this. The scowl on his face said he wanted to punch something.

After dropping his case by the table with a *thunk*, shrugging off his jacket and flinging it over a chair, he crossed behind the bench and kissed her—a long, penetrating appetiser that, despite her unease at his current humour, left her hungry for more. His strong arms finally released her, and Sophie inhaled deeply at the line etched between his brows, and the shadows in his usually bright blue eyes. What was bothering him so much?

Her stomach pitched.

Her own bit of news would only make his mood worse.

'I missed you so much today,' he murmured, on a seductive but weary grin.

Sophie was about to ask what was wrong, when he spun away and grabbed an apple from between the overripe bananas in the china fruit bowl.

He cast a look around. 'Where's Paige?' He chomped into the Granny Smith, then flicked her daggy apron's hem. '*Very* sexy, by the way.'

She glowed inside. That one wicked smile was worth the cleaning-up time. She'd answer his question, then get to the bottom of his trouble. 'Your sister's upstairs, doing homework,' she said, collecting her knife to chop another carrot.

Cooper set the apple on the bench. 'Homework on a Friday night?' He circled her back, then came in for a nerve-tingling snuggle against her neck. 'You teachers don't cut them much slack. They only landed back in the country a couple of days ago.'

They'd collected Paige at the airport on Wednesday. She'd been exhausted, but beaming and full of stories and plans to go back to France. On the drive home Cooper had explained that Sophie and he spent lots of time together these days, which included sleepovers. Paige hadn't batted an eyelid except to say, 'Excellent!'

His fresh apple breath brushed her ear, and she hugged tight a wonderful inner warmth. This living together wasn't so bad. Not so bad at all.

'Why don't you have a night off cooking?' he said. 'We'll get takeout.' He nipped her lobe. 'I feel like chilli dogs and fries.'

Sophie almost gagged. Midway through her second trimester, any sign of morning sickness had passed—but chilli turned her stomach at the best of times.

He manoeuvred her around. 'We could snuggle up together under a big soft blanket on the couch.' His eyes flashed. 'Hey, there's a big game on tonight.' The alarm must have shown on her face. He arched a brow. 'Of course I'm sure there's a romantic comedy that I'd happily sit and watch with you.'

He was being so considerate. What was she supposed to do? He hated most rom-coms. She hated football. But she didn't want to give up the opportunity to snuggle with the man of her dreams. Because that was what Cooper Smith had become—had been, she now realised, from the moment he'd asked her to dance. How long did it usually take to fall in love? All she knew was that after these weeks spent together, she was there.

Today's pile of mail caught his eye. He collected the stash and filtered through. 'Any news from Myers today?'

Sophie held her breath.

As a matter of fact...

She positioned three shallots and cut off their heads. 'He invited me into his office. He didn't ask for my resignation but he *did* say that he'd heard about my...' she paused '...*situation* from another teacher, and looked forward to hearing about a wedding—as would all the Unity girls and their paying parents.'

Cooper lowered the envelopes. 'That's laying his cards on the table. What did you tell him?'

His eyes glittered a message.

This is showtime, Sophie. What are you going to do?

Groaning, she chopped the shallots again.

What *was* she going to do? She loved teaching at Unity. She loved her girls. However, despite setting out to keep her heart safe, she had fallen in love with Cooper. She was smitten by everything about him. Not only that, as the weeks rolled on she felt increasingly lucky that he obviously cared for her too.

So why didn't he tell her?

'Hey, guys.' Paige, in her long orange fleecy-lined PJs, came breezing in. Stopping in her tracks, she played with a frown. 'Has he got you cooking again?' She continued on, slippers slapping on the heated tiles. 'I say strike!'

Sophie watched Cooper skate looks between the two women in his life. The penny dropped, and she held her breath, predicting his next words. Was he going to tell Paige about the baby? Last night she'd agreed with him that it was time, but she wasn't nearly prepared enough for it *now*.

'Paige,' he said, 'we need to have a talk about Sophie and me…and you.'

Sophie could barely draw a breath. Oh, God. This

was it. He was going to tell Paige she would soon be an auntie. Would he then require an answer from her about her place at Unity?

Sophie dropped the knife on the counter and her palm went to her stomach.

This didn't feel right. They should be sitting together after dinner, relaxed, with Cooper in a better mood. Maybe tomorrow. Not now.

Decided, Sophie removed her apron and placed it next to the knife. 'Cooper, can I see you for a minute?'

He didn't seem to hear, but moved over to where Paige had hitched up onto a kitchen stool.

'Honey, you know Sophie and I are going out?'

Paige's brow crinkled. She stole a piece of carrot and popped it into her mouth. 'Yeah. So?'

Cooper propped a hip over the stool nearest Paige. The strong planes of his face shifted as he concentrated—no doubt on finding the right words. 'We like each other a lot.'

Paige's pretty face lit up. 'Really? I didn't notice.'

'So much, in fact…' He took a moment. Lowered his voice to an earnest timbre. 'Well, we're having a baby.'

Sophie closed her eyes. She heard Paige gasp, then exclaim, 'You. Are. *Kidding* me.'

Knotted up inside, Sophie sneaked open one eye. The snowball was rolling. No turning back now. By Tuesday next week the whole school would know, and Grumble-bum Myers would rush her in and insist upon an answer. The principal would never say it out loud, but she knew what the subtext would be: find a husband or leave my school.

Cooper's large hand cupped Paige's on the bench. 'We're due early next year.'

Paige dropped her head back and hooted at the ceiling. 'That is the coolest thing I have *ever* heard! I'm going to be an aunt, and go to college the same year.' She jumped up and hugged Cooper, then scooted around to embrace Sophie, who discovered she was smiling through a smear of tears. At least Paige was accepting of the situation. At the end of the day, wasn't that more important than a job?

Paige stepped back and scrutinised Sophie's tummy. Her mouth swung to one side. 'Well, I guess you've got a minor bump happening.' She clasped her hands under her chin and bounced up and down. 'Can I babysit? Pretty please? I'll make myself available practically all the time.'

Cooper laughed and stood up tall. 'You can babysit anytime you like.' He looked to Sophie with the same kind of relief she felt swimming in her eyes. 'Isn't that right, sweetheart?'

Sophie's grandparents were gorgeous, but she'd never felt as connected as she'd have liked with her own parents. With these two special people, however, she seemed to have found that missing piece. A little weird to accept it so quickly, but also entirely wonderful.

She belonged here—she and her baby both. What could matter more than that?

Pretending to be stern, Cooper joined them. 'Just

don't get any clucky ideas of your own, Paige. This is a special situation, not an example to follow. I know how much you love babies.' He dug a thumb into his sister's ribs to make her laugh. 'I'll have to keep an extra-watchful eye on you now.'

Paige's pupils dilated. She opened her mouth, shut it, then spoke up. 'Actually, I need to talk to you about something too.' She took a gulp of air, then rushed the words out. 'I want to invite someone over.'

Sophie fell back against the bench. *It was all happening.*

Last night, before lights out, she and Paige had discussed how they should broach the subject of introducing Hallam to the family. But tonight wasn't the time for Cooper to hear about boyfriends—particularly given his less than subtle warning just now, and his dark face earlier.

She hadn't even had a chance to tell him yet about the invitation she'd received today from an old friend to her wedding in Perth. He was so protective, so cautious about the baby's well-being, how would he react to her flying to the west coast of Australia when she was even further along?

Cooper smiled at Paige. 'You want to invite someone over? Who is it? A new friend from school? Someone you bonded with when you were away?'

When Paige hesitated, Sophie gripped the edge of the counter. She couldn't bear the suspense.

Paige finally squeaked out, 'It's my boyfriend.'

Cooper's positive expression slid off his face.

Paige didn't back down. 'His name is Hallam Gregson, and he wants to meet you.'

Cooper remained still. 'How long have you known him?'

Paige lifted her chin. 'Six months.'

Cooper coughed out a humourless laugh and then, waving his hands, walked away. 'No. Uh-uh. I don't think so.'

'Cooper, why not?' Sophie stopped herself. Should she have spoken? Was this between Cooper and his sister? Should she butt out?

But on second thoughts she believed she *should* intervene. Paige might be younger, but they were still friends. While she sympathised with Cooper's need to protect, this was going overboard, and someone needed to say so.

Cooper slowly faced her. 'Why not, Sophie? Simple. Because it's best. She's too young to be getting serious with boys. *Way* too young.'

His parents had died and left him with the responsibility of bringing up his baby sister. He was used to being in charge; he'd had to be. Cooper was the only guardian Paige had, and he'd taken that duty seriously. Sophie must keep that at the forefront of her mind now, as she tried to explain.

She kept her voice level and calm. 'Paige is almost seventeen.' She tried on a smile. 'I might think something was wrong if she *didn't* have a boyfriend by this time.'

His jaw tightened. 'Bringing up a teenager isn't as easy as it looks.'

Grinning, she rolled her eyes. 'You're preaching to the converted, remember?'

His face didn't crack. 'You're Paige's teacher, *not* her mother.'

The blow hit Sophie like a medicine ball to the stomach. Emotion stung the back of her throat and her mouth felt too rubbery to answer—even if she could think of something half-intelligent to say.

Cooper's eyes flooded with something that vaguely resembled guilt before he turned to poor Paige. 'So, is this the situation Sophie told me about?'

Sophie withered. Oh, God. That sounded bad.

With pleading eyes, Sophie shook her head at Paige. 'I didn't tell him anything.'

But Paige's face had crumpled. She took a step back. 'You...told him?'

'No. Well...yes. But not how you think.' That first night together, after the wedding, she'd offhandedly mentioned a girl at school who had a boyfriend putting pressure on her. While Sophie had deflected Cooper's questions in the Italian restaurant weeks later, Cooper had obviously put it together now.

Paige didn't stay to listen. 'I can't believe I *trusted* you!' She fled the room, one slipper left behind in the dash.

Her stomach on the floor, Sophie began to follow—then held back. Paige needed time to cool off. And *she* needed time to sort out how she would explain this mess. Would Paige believe that she hadn't betrayed her confidence? How could she ever convince her? Would Paige ever trust her again?

Sophie found little comfort in Cooper's voice at her back. His comment about her not being Paige's mother still echoed in her brain. So much for feeling like family.

He groaned, then cursed himself—and then again. 'I didn't handle that very well, did I?'

She made an uncomplimentary noise. 'You stank.'

He turned her around and set her chin on the crook of his finger. 'I'll go up and apologise.'

Hope soared. But she wasn't totally convinced. She probed his gaze. 'You mean you'll meet Paige's boyfriend?'

A series of shadows crossed over his face, then he shrugged. 'Seems I can't hold back the sands of time.' He brushed back her hair. 'Besides, it'll give me a chance to lay down the law. Better than needing a shotgun later.'

Sophie cringed. 'That's not funny.'

Cooper's eyes hardened. 'It wasn't meant to be.'

She wanted to bring up his 'not her mother' comment, but now that he'd given in Sophie felt it might be better to live and let live. However, she did want to know what had upset him before coming home. Plus she needed to talk to him about that wedding invitation. Not a pleasant thought.

Before she could say any of it, Cooper pressed a kiss to her brow and strode away.

'I'll go get hot dogs. You stay here and talk to Paige. Tell her I'm a bastard—but a bastard who loves her and only wants to keep her safe.'

As he collected his jacket and moved out of the room, Sophie blew out a breath.

One tiny cowardly part of her wanted to throw up her hands and say, *Sorry, this is all too hard*. But that was not an option; she was having Cooper's baby. And yet that wasn't the deciding factor in keeping her here, wanting to help and support.

She was in love with Cooper. She also loved Paige—maybe one day soon as much as the sister she'd never had.

Finding a much needed smile, Sophie set to work sweeping up the chopped veggies.

She guessed she was getting married.

CHAPTER THIRTEEN

SOPHIE sat at a Darling Harbour *al fresco* table, a gorgeous meal before her and the world's most handsome man at her side. The night lights from the city spilled shimmering pools of blue and gold over the calm water. Families, couples and singles strolled by, taking advantage of the crisp evening air and the attractions this buzzing tourist site was famous for.

The atmosphere should have been perfect, and it would be—as soon as Sophie had told Cooper the news she had sat on for close to two weeks. After that blowout with Paige, the time hadn't seemed right. But time had run out.

Her fork toyed around her salad. She took a breath, put on a smile and searched out his gaze. *Here goes.*

'Did I mention I'd received an invitation to a friend's wedding? We were best friends in primary school but lost touch for a while.'

Smiling back, Cooper set down his cutlery. 'Great. Is a partner invited?' She nodded. He patted his mouth with a napkin. 'Where and when?'

'In a month.' She straightened the napkin in her lap. 'In Perth.'

His brows opened up. He blinked. 'You want to drive?'

She shot out a laugh. 'Of course not. Perth's well over three thousand kilometres from Sydney.'

He studied her face for a protracted awkward moment that sent a shiver of apprehension shooting up her backbone. He looked down and started cutting his steak. 'You shouldn't fly while you're pregnant.'

Her fist closed around her napkin. 'Unless I have a condition, no airline or doctor would suggest I not fly.'

His knife cluttered down. '*I'm* suggesting it.'

These past weeks her belief that she'd fallen in love with Cooper had only increased. At times the depth of her feelings almost frightened her. Despite her hesitation in agreeing to this arrangement, now she truly wanted this to work. Her child was Cooper's child too. She'd tried to understand and accommodate his over-protective nature, but telling her she shouldn't fly was over the top.

She'd been so pleased when he'd finally come around to realising that, at almost seventeen, Paige should be entitled to date—even if Cooper *was* delaying making a date to have Hallam Gregson over. Thank heaven Paige had listened when Sophie had explained that she hadn't betrayed her confidence. The two of them were back to being buddies— though Sophie knew Paige wasn't nearly as open with her as she once had been.

Sophie collected her fork and fiddled with her cos lettuce and cherry tomatoes while Cooper waited for an answer. Finally she left her food and sat back. 'I'm sorry, Cooper, but that's not good enough. If you don't want me to fly, you'll have to give me a good reason.'

Her unspoken words hung in the air.

I'm going to the wedding, no matter what you say.

She didn't want to argue, but she couldn't be a doormat either. Her days of docile conformity were gone, and nothing could bring them back. Not even the displeasure radiating from Cooper's eyes now.

Finally breaking his gaze, he set his jaw, found the salt and seasoned his potato. 'I have my reasons.'

'Then let me hear them.' The tension stretching between them was palpable, but she wouldn't— *couldn't*—back down.

He tugged an ear, then pushed his plate aside.

'When I was eight,' he began in a low voice, 'my mother fell pregnant—another boy, apparently. With four months to go, she accompanied my father to an international accountants' conference. On the return trip she experienced pain. She lost the baby, and nearly her own life, just hours after landing back in Australia.'

The blood in Sophie's head tingled, then rushed to her feet. She gripped the table-edge to stop from sliding to the ground. In her mind's eye she saw *her* baby, *her* life. In four weeks, when she planned to fly to Perth, she'd have four months to go too.

Cooper grasped her hand. 'My mother lay in her

room for what seemed like months after the miscarriage. I won't take the slightest risk of you suffering the same fate.'

Or risk his own loss and pain, which she understood.

Sophie slanted her head and leant forward. 'But they couldn't have blamed the miscarriage on the fact that she'd flown.' Unless his mother had had a condition of which she and her doctor had been unaware.

'They didn't discount it either.' Cooper seemed about to explain more when his gaze wandered to the left. He squinted, then blinked several times, before his shoulders drew slowly back.

He scraped back his steel-framed chair and pushed to his feet. 'Wasn't Paige supposed to be staying over at Marlo's tonight?'

Sophie nodded—then comprehension dawned with the blinding power of a supernova.

Frowning, Cooper scrubbed a hand over his jaw, then strode off. Panic exploded through Sophie's system as she spun to check.

Paige stood by Darling Harbour's swirling spiral fountain, kissing Hallam Gregson.

Oh, Lord.

Sophie grabbed her handbag and caught up with Cooper at the same time he caught up with the teens.

Cooper didn't pull them apart. No need. Hallam must have sensed the older man's looming shadow. The youth, dressed in dark blue jeans and a pressed dress shirt, turned his head, peered into Cooper's fierce gaze and broke the kiss. But not the embrace.

Eyes closed, Paige, in a pretty yellow skirt, was still in la-la land.

Hallam whispered into her ear. 'I think I'm about to meet your brother.'

Paige's eyes sprang open and she jumped. 'Coop!'

Cooper set his fists on his hips. 'You are grounded for a month. *Then* you're grounded for another month.'

Sophie soothed his steaming back. Beneath his light jumper, Cooper was on fire.

Face ashen, Paige made stop signs with her hands. 'I can explain.'

'You can do that tomorrow. Now you're coming home with us.' He went to grab her arm, but Paige dodged.

Her expression was set. 'I'm staying with Hallam, and there's nothing you can do about it.'

Hallam spoke up. 'Mr Smith, sir, if we can just sit down somewhere, I think I can—'

Cooper's head snapped to the right. 'I'm not talking to you, son.' He spoke to Paige. 'It's dark. These streets can be dangerous. I thought you were at Marlo's. What if you'd got mugged? Or worse?'

Paige edged closer, her face almost tranquil now. 'But I'm with Hallam.' She looped her arm through her boyfriend's, and Hallam smiled at her in a way that assured Sophie their feelings were mutual. 'He would never let anything happen to me.'

Cooper groaned. 'Haven't I taught you anything? You have to control yourself and *think*. Think of your future, what you're doing—and in *public*, for Pete's sake.'

Hallam stood up tall. 'I love your sister, Mr Smith.'

Cooper slid him a jaded look. 'I was your age once. I'm sure you think you do.'

Sophie set a protective arm around Paige. 'That's enough, Cooper.'

'You *bet* it's enough.' Tears of frustration flooding her eyes, Paige pulled away. 'We can run away if we want. We can *elope*. We don't have to follow your stupid rules, Cooper. I'm sick to *death* of them!'

People had slowed up to listen and talk behind their hands. Cooper didn't notice. 'Rules are necessary.' His hand sliced down on each beat. 'Rules are about order and safety.'

'They're *your* rules. Not mine. And I'm not going to feel like a prisoner anymore.' Bursting into tears, Paige ran off towards the water. Her young Romeo shot after her.

Cooper smacked his forehead and trod a tight, frustrated circle. 'She's going to run off and get married. Have a baby or two. I'll be a grandfather before I'm thirty-five.'

Despite it all, Sophie grinned. *Grandfather?* He meant uncle…

She went to him. 'I don't think they'll elope. But they do need to be heard. And to have their feelings appreciated.' Cooper could sometimes forget about such things. 'We should trust Paige enough to hope she'll make the right, informed decisions.'

He studied her hard. 'Did you suggest the elopement?'

She sucked down a breath. '*What?* Of course I didn't.'

He took a moment to accept that, then shoved his hands in his pockets. 'Well, I don't want you two discussing this business again. She's heard enough. And *seen* enough. Next thing she'll be thinking it's totally *acceptable* to go and fall pregnant.'

As a chill crept down her spine, Sophie looked at him and swore she saw the mask of Hyde.

Was that what Cooper really thought? That she'd *planned* to conceive that night? Did he think she'd tried to pull Evangeline's trick to 'get her man'?

Despite two years of dating, he hadn't fallen in love with Evangeline. Sophie had begun to wonder if he would ever profess those words to her. If he was in love with her, as she now loved him, why didn't he say?

Beyond that, tonight she'd realised that her right to make decisions was indeed being manipulated away. It wasn't about whether she stayed in her job, or if she went to the wedding, it was about Cooper's belief that he would make decisions for her because he *should* and *could*.

Just like Paige, Sophie didn't want to be dependent on Cooper and his rules. She didn't want to be dependent on anyone. She wanted her opinion to matter. Dammit, *she* wanted to matter. And matter to a man who *loved* her.

Burgeoning emotion stung her nose and eyes. Pressing her lips together, Sophie willed the threat of tears away. She refused to mindlessly comply, or explain herself for the next however many years. And she refused to bring her child up in a household with backbiting parents.

Garnering her inner strength, Sophie spun on her heel and headed for the main street to find a taxi rank.

Cooper's deep voice boomed after her. 'Sophie, we're talking.'

Her heartbeat tripping madly in her chest, she increased her pace. She was done talking.

He strode up and barred her way. Wrong move. If he wanted a confrontation, he'd better be ready for one.

Swallowing against the lump wedged in her throat, Sophie threw up her hands. 'We've been kidding ourselves, Cooper. Right from the start. We're good in bed, but that's about it.'

His face grew darker before he pulled her into a quiet alcove, away from the curious crowd. 'We'll talk about this when we get home.'

No dice. 'I'm glad we tried. It was *right* to try. But I'm not going to force myself on you, and I certainly won't allow you to force your rules onto me.' A hot tear slid down her cheek. 'It's better that the baby has two parents who live separately than a married couple who disagree all the time. And not only on what TV programme to watch or who's going to cook, but on fundamental issues.'

A hand rushed through his hair, leaving it in

spikes. 'We have the same ethics and moral code. We established that weeks ago.'

'So you don't want more than one partner, you wouldn't cheat or steal, and you'd rather try to save another human being than see them die. That's great. But those hypotheticals don't apply to us here, now, *tonight*.'

Another tear trailed down her face, curling around her chin, and she trembled.

She hugged herself to stop the shaking, the avalanche of pain. 'You're trying to keep Paige pegged in, but you're only succeeding in pushing her away. And I couldn't stand by and be the dutiful wife if you tried to do the same with this child.' Her lungs clogged with suffocating emotion. 'I'd end up hating you.'

'We could never hate each other.' He brought her into him, determined, uncompromising. 'We belong together. We're a family.'

Rather than giving in to the warmth and the strength, Sophie closed her eyes and tried desperately to find some calm place deep inside.

She met his gaze, so close she wanted to kiss him, not let him go. 'I want to be part of a family. *Our* family. But not enough to throw away my principles and my pride.'

She spotted Paige crying in the distance. How she wanted to go to her. But Hallam was there, holding her and smoothing her hair. It wasn't her place to interfere. Not anymore.

'Your sister needs you,' she told him. 'And in a loving, supportive way or don't bother.' She squirmed out of his arms.

He gripped her hand. 'This isn't over, Sophie.'

'You can stop looking.' Heart breaking in two, she freed her hand and walked away. 'No rainbow happening here. Please, Cooper, just let it go.'

CHAPTER FOURTEEN

BUT he hadn't been able to let Sophie go that night—one more nail in his coffin.

A month later, slumped outside in what had once been his favourite corner of the world, Cooper threw a ragged tennis ball at the slate ground the opposite end of the goldfish pond. It bounced on the slate, then against the rendered wall, and he caught it for perhaps the hundredth time that night.

Which equalled the number of mistakes he'd made with Sophie.

He tossed the ball again. *Thump-thump*, catch.

One. He'd seduced her when he'd given his word he wouldn't.

Two. He'd talked her into living with him when she'd told him plain and simple she did not want marriage.

Three. He hadn't respected her decisions about the baby enough to really listen. The stairs, the air travel, her wish to continue working.

Thump-thump, catch.

He'd treated Sophie in much the same way he'd treated Paige. But Sophie wasn't a young girl. Hell, neither was Paige anymore.

Mistake number four. Not acknowledging that his baby sister had grown up into a young woman.

He slumped lower in the deckchair, legs wide apart, his beard growth three days old.

Focusing inward, he squeezed the ball in his dangling hand.

If he had to put one word to his problem, he could. Fear. Fear of what had happened—of what *could* happen. He should have grabbed joy with both hands and tossed it up into the air, knowing that if he and Sophie failed to catch it, at least they'd have had some fun and known some happiness along the way.

When his lawyer friend had told him the other week that his wife had miscarried and lost their longed-for baby, Cooper had felt sick to his gut. He should have discussed it with Sophie, but he'd buried it that night and let it fester, making his determination to protect her and their baby all the more exaggerated.

His leaden arm lifted.

Thump-thump, catch.

It had been hard, but he'd mended his fences with Paige and her boyfriend...

Hallam Gregson. Hallam.

Nice enough boy too.

Cooper growled. *Young man.* Eighteen wasn't a boy. And, like it or not, he'd have to let Paige go and spend time with her beau, so she could fly back to him if ever she needed to.

He ground his teeth and sucked in the mock-orange scent that reminded him of times spent out here with Sophie.

He'd demanded she not walk the streets of Sydney that night in search of a cab. Insisted she come home with him. They'd dropped Hallam off while Paige had sat sullen and silent in the back seat. When they'd arrived home, his tear-streaked sister had stormed off to her room, Sophie had said goodnight, and in the morning she'd been gone.

Not even a note.

He'd sent flowers, shown up on her doorstep. He'd very briefly thought of throwing pebbles at her window and waxing romantic in the moonlight. But that wouldn't have worked either.

However, he *would* get her back—even if right now he was completely stumped over how to achieve that.

About to move inside, Cooper spied a movement in the bushes. A frog? A snake?

A pair of what looked like reflectors appeared, glowing and blinking out from the darkness. A moment later a cat glided through the leaves. A black cat with big green eyes.

Cooper's heart beat faster. He hunched over, fingers rubbing together as if offering a treat.

'Here, kitty.'

Long tail shot high, the cat wound around. Sat to lick its paw. Then sashayed over.

Cooper smiled. 'That's a good kitty. You must know I'm feeling lonely.' *And stupid and—*

As easily as she'd decided to approach, the cat decided to leave again. Halfway to his hand, it turned and padded away.

Cooper knew a flash of irrational panic. What had Sophie said he should do? Pat its head three times or it was bad luck? He probably needed to get up and follow. Ridiculous. Really very dumb.

He pushed up.

But he couldn't let it go.

As if hearing, the cat swung around and came near enough to curl itself around his leg.

Cooper exhaled, chuckled, and gently eased it up onto his lap. As she started up a purr and clawed his lap, preparing for a nap, the answer came to Cooper as clear and colourful as the rainbow Sophie no longer believed in.

He stroked the cat's head—once, twice, three times.

He knew what to do to get Sophie back. But he'd need more than a little luck to succeed.

CHAPTER FIFTEEN

CHEEK embedded in her palm, Sophie sat watching the smiling happy couples dance and laugh around the wedding reception dance floor.

Smiling.

Happy.

Wedding.

Sophie groaned. She had never felt more like crying in her life.

Not that it hadn't been a beautiful day. The bride was gorgeous. The groom so proud. Wonderful flowers. Delicious food—though she'd eaten very little.

She'd bought her ticket, boarded the plane and had found her own way here. She hadn't needed to try and please anyone but herself.

What a big fat joke.

Inhaling deeply, she sat back and rubbed her growing belly. Horrible to admit, but the only joy she knew right now was feeling her baby move inside her.

She already loved her child. Just as she loved his father—so desperately, so deeply, some mornings she could barely drag herself out of bed for the lingering memories of vivid dreams. But get out of bed she must.

She needed her job, and with grumble-bum Myers sacked for undisclosed reasons by the board—the head of which was switched-on and lived in the twenty-first century—Sophie's position at Unity was once again secure.

Another victory. Yet it felt hollow.

Sophie leaned forward and poured herself more water.

At least she still got to see Paige five days a week until the end of the year. It seemed she and Cooper had worked out their differences. Over the last month Paige and Hallam had been seeing each other openly; anxious talk of moving out and eloping no longer featured in Paige's conversation. She guessed Cooper had realised his mistake—that if he tried to control his sister he would likely lose her. Sophie was happy for Paige. At least one of them had got their happy ending.

The rock 'n' roll number blasting from the speakers faded out as the DJ's voice faded up.

'Almost time to wind up this fabulous evening, folks,' the DJ crooned. 'But before we play our last dance number, here's a special request to satisfy all those espionage flick fans. We're taking you way back to 1977. Enjoy, and remember.'

Sophie collected her handbag and pushed up from the otherwise vacant round table. She'd reserved a hotel suite near the top floor, with a view of Perth's Swan River. A silly indulgence, but if she couldn't have Cooper at least for tonight she could do all she could to reinvent as many memories as possible.

About to head for the door, she recognised the polished tune that had begun to play. "The Spy Who Loved Me." Her chest clutched with inconsolable longing, but still she smiled. An oldie, and the perfect song to fire up visions of her own perfect James Bond. But as the tune swelled, Sophie felt so gripped by emotion she worried she might not be able to dam the tears about to break.

She would never love anyone like she loved him. But at least she would see Cooper regularly. She'd have her baby. Their baby.

She felt a kick inside and her hand covered the spot, caressing. This little one would always know there'd been no mistakes as far as he was concerned.

As she turned to leave, her lucky bracelet snagged on the chair's silver ribbon. The clasp slipped open for the first time ever and it fell.

Sophie barely had time to think, *This must be bad luck; that means it's definitely over,* before a large dark masculine figure swooped and caught the bracelet before it hit the ground.

Unable to breathe, cheeks suddenly on fire, Sophie waited as the man, dressed in a splendid tuxedo, straightened and issued a knee-knocking smile.

He lowered his head to her ear. She shivered at the familiar hot scent and the smooth sable voice when he murmured, 'This is definitely our dance.'

Sophie almost crumpled. But she wouldn't allow

it. She hadn't changed her mind about Cooper. About marrying him. About returning to the compliant 'yes' girl she'd used to be. She most definitely, absolutely had not.

Without permission he took her hand, led her out onto the dance floor and pressed her gently in. A tremor of pleasure and desire shuddered through her. Sophie thought over the situation for what seemed an eternity before resting her cheek gingerly against his chest. Instantly she melted into the heat.

It was a wedding, after all, and only one dance. No reason to be uncivil, since he'd come all this way.

His voice rumbled against her ear. 'I came here tonight to admit I was wrong and you were right. I'm arrogant and pushy, and we have next to nothing in common.' He swirled her round, his chin resting lightly on her crown. 'Yes, it is true that we're incredibly compatible in the bedroom—which, I might add, was a very good point you made the other week.'

She grinned. Just had to get that in, didn't he?

'But the question is,' he went on, 'is that enough for two people to build a life on? I wanted to believe it was. But, as I said, I was wrong.'

He was *wrong*?

But while her mind swirled, and she wondered what would come next, her body didn't care about words that confused her. Her blood only knew that now she was warm. Her heart only understood that this minute she was no longer lonely.

Which meant one thing. She must pull away from Cooper's deadly charm before it was too late.

Somehow finding the strength, she wrangled out of his hold. She planted her feet, raised her chin. 'It won't work, Cooper. Not this time.'

His eyes crinkled and a smile hooked up one side of his mouth. 'You look lovely in that dress. Long and satiny. I didn't know a woman could wear white to a wedding unless she was the bride.'

'Times have changed. Women have choices now.'

Nothing subtle about that subtext.

His voice lowered, barely audible over the music. 'A black cat visited me last night. It was a sign.'

Sophie shook her head. 'You don't believe in superstition. You've told me again and again.'

His eyes darkened as he found her hands and held them tight. 'You believe in luck. I believe in fate. Last night I realised none of that matters. Because all we need to do is believe in each other.'

She was shaking her head again, but tears prickled behind her eyes. 'No, Cooper. *No*. You'd want to make all the decisions, and I'd be constantly explaining myself, and then you'd get your own way regardless.'

It didn't matter how or why he was like that; that was simply the way Cooper was. In charge.

Sophie blinked.

Although he *had* come around with Paige finally…

'I'm sorry,' Cooper said. 'For everything. To say I acted the way I did because I care isn't enough, I know. But if giving *us* a go wasn't a wrong or a bad idea, can't we at least give it one more shot?'

The battle raging inside her became stronger, fiercer. The more it intensified, the more she wanted to say yes. Wanted to believe in the rainbow. But it wasn't that easy. She'd promised herself no more Get Out of Jail Free cards. 'You can apologise, but nothing's changed.'

'Things *have* changed.'

A stab of hope crossed with despair pierced her heart, and she had to look away. This hurt too much. She didn't have to put herself through it. Not again. 'I told you to let me go that night and I meant it. Can't you please just respect my decision?' *Respect me?*

The music faded out and another song started. The disco ball began to slowly spin, throwing rotating dots of purple light over everyone and everything.

He tilted her chin and spoke to her eyes, as if willing his words to penetrate and bury deep.

'Things will be different—I know they will. Because…I love you, Sophie. I do. And I know you love me too.'

A sob of pain—relief, disbelief—was wrenched up from her very soul. He wasn't playing fair. Did he truly mean it? Or was it simply a way to get her and his child back? Could he be that manipulative? That cruel?

'We were lucky enough to find each other,' he said, pulling in her shoulders, urging her closer to his mesmerising will and his way-too-kissable mouth.

'We can't throw it away just because we're not brave enough to try again.'

She shook her head—she shouldn't listen. But he continued, his heart in his eyes.

'Think of me as a drowning man. I won't pull you under, but I do need your help. I need you, Sophie Schoolteacher, and you need me. We need each other because we're family. Now. Always.'

Right or wrong, every fibre of her being cried out to fling her arms around him and never let him go, no matter what. Her stomach pitched. She couldn't crumple. She had to at least try to shrug it off.

She feigned a nonchalant face and coughed out a laugh. 'Is that all you've got?'

'No.' He retrieved a small crimson jewellery box from his jacket's inside pocket and snapped open the lid. 'I have this.'

Struck dumb, Sophie blinked at the unbelievable sparkle, so bright and special he might have caught a handful of stars and placed them in there just for her. But as she came nearer she knew the truth. Stars were close; inside that box was the most beautiful diamond ring she'd ever seen.

And the design!

She gasped. 'Is that three *butterflies* over the band?'

He slipped the ring out and slotted the box back in his pocket. 'It's not an engagement ring.'

Sophie's heart plummeted. 'Oh?'

He took her hand and slid it on her finger before she could protest. Well, truth to tell, she was so surprised and delighted she didn't want to object. Suddenly all the fight had gone out of her, vanished like a magician's trick, to be replaced with hope—real hope—and more love than she could possibly handle.

He loved her? Really? This wasn't a scam or a dream?

She looked closer. He'd placed the ring on her wedding finger. 'If it's not an engagement ring...'

'It's an eternity ring. The three butterflies are for luck, like you said. The white diamonds are of the highest purity and the band is white gold. But the jeweller said if you weren't happy—'

'Cooper?'

His head tipped forward. 'Yes, sweetheart?'

She allowed a smile, which unfurled from around her heart. 'You can stop explaining now.'

His own brilliant smile broke and two strong arms looped over her head. He drew her near for the kiss of the millennium, but hesitated. 'Just checking. Does that mean yes?'

A tear ran down her cheek as she nodded. 'It also means I love you too.'

Gently he brushed back a curl. 'For the rest of our lives?'

She held his hand to her face. 'Much longer than that.'

He kissed her deeply, with everything she knew he was, and wanted to be, and wanted to give. When they resurfaced she half expected the wedding reception crowd to applaud. But each couple on the dance floor seemed to be in a similar intimate zone.

Cooper rocked her gently to the music, but his eyes didn't leave hers. 'We'll start organising as soon as we get back. You wanted a wedding on the beach.'

He remembered? And he was okay with it? 'I thought you'd want a traditional church wedding.'

'I want you.' He waltzed her around. 'Do you know how happy we're going to be, Sophie Smith?'

Sophie dissolved with joy.

Sophie Smith sounded so right. *Felt* so right.

Grinning, she tugged her sexy soul mate's tie. Before his mouth slanted over hers again, she murmured, 'I think I have a good idea.'

Undressed
BY THE BOSS

From sensible suits...into satin sheets!

Even if at times work is rather boring, there is one
person making the office a whole lot more interesting:
the boss! He's in control, he knows what he wants and
he's going to get it! He's tall, handsome, breathtakingly
attractive. And there's one outcome that's never in
doubt—the heroines of these electrifying, supersexy
stories will be undressed by the boss!

*A brand-new miniseries available only from
Harlequin Presents!*

Available in August:

TAKEN BY THE
MAVERICK MILLIONAIRE
by *Anna Cleary*
Book # 2754

In September, don't miss another breathtaking boss in

THE TYCOON'S VERY
PERSONAL ASSISTANT
by *Heidi Rice*

www.eHarlequin.com

HP12754

I ♥ HARLEQUIN® *Presents~*

BROUGHT TO YOU BY FANS OF HARLEQUIN PRESENTS.

We are its editors and authors
and biggest fans—and we'd
love to hear from YOU!

Subscribe today to our online blog at
www.iheartpresents.com

REQUEST YOUR FREE BOOKS!

HARLEQUIN® *Presents* ®

2 FREE NOVELS PLUS 2 FREE GIFTS!

PASSION GUARANTEED SEDUCTION

YES! Please send me 2 FREE Harlequin Presents® novels and my 2 FREE gifts (gifts are worth about $10). After receiving them, if I don't wish to receive any more books, I can return the shipping statement marked "cancel". If I don't cancel, I will receive 6 brand-new novels every month and be billed just $4.05 per book in the U.S. or $4.74 per book in Canada, plus 25¢ shipping and handling per book and applicable taxes, if any*. That's a savings of close to 15% off the cover price! I understand that accepting the 2 free books and gifts places me under no obligation to buy anything. I can always return a shipment and cancel at any time. Even if I never buy another book, the two free books and gifts are mine to keep forever.

106 HDN ERRW 306 HDN ERRL

Name   (PLEASE PRINT)

Address   Apt. #

City   State/Prov.   Zip/Postal Code

Signature (if under 18, a parent or guardian must sign)

Mail to the Harlequin Reader Service:
IN U.S.A.: P.O. Box 1867, Buffalo, NY 14240-1867
IN CANADA: P.O. Box 609, Fort Erie, Ontario L2A 5X3

Not valid to current subscribers of Harlequin Presents books.

Want to try two free books from another line?
Call 1-800-873-8635 or visit www.morefreebooks.com.

* Terms and prices subject to change without notice. N.Y. residents add applicable sales tax. Canadian residents will be charged applicable provincial taxes and GST. Offer not valid in Quebec. This offer is limited to one order per household. All orders subject to approval. Credit or debit balances in a customer's account(s) may be offset by any other outstanding balance owed by or to the customer. Please allow 4 to 6 weeks for delivery. Offer available while quantities last.

Your Privacy: Harlequin Books is committed to protecting your privacy. Our Privacy Policy is available online at www.eHarlequin.com or upon request from the Reader Service. From time to time we make our lists of customers available to reputable third parties who may have a product or service of interest to you. If you would prefer we not share your name and address, please check here. ☐

HP08R

LAURA WRIGHT

FRONT PAGE ENGAGEMENT

Media mogul and playboy Trent Tanford is
being blackmailed *and* he's involved in a
scandal. Needing to shed his image, Trent
marries his girl-next-door neighbor,
Carrie Gray, with some major cash tossed
her way. Carrie accepts for her own reasons,
but falls in love with Trent and wonders
if he could feel the same way about her—
even though their mock marriage was,
after all, just a business deal.

**Available August
wherever books are sold.**

Always Powerful, Passionate and Provocative.